GOODNIGHT STORIES

ISBN 0 86112 144 9
© BRIMAX RIGHTS 1982 All rights reserved
First Published by BRIMAX BOOKS, ENGLAND 1982.
This revised edition published in 1983.
Third Printing 1984.
The stories in this collection have also
appeared in four titles BEDTIME SERIES
All published by Brimax Books
Printed in Hong Kong

GOODNIGHT STORIES

Illustrated by

Gerry Embleton and Pamela Storey

BRIMAX BOOKS·CAMBRIDGE·ENGLAND

CONTENTS

AROUND THE WORLD IN AN AFTERNOON

Jonathin Spindle was tall and thin and very long. He had long legs, long arms, long feet and a long nose. One day, when he had nothing else to do, he put some bread and cheese into a paper bag and said,

"I shall walk round the world today."

He pointed his long feet towards the door.

"When you know where you are going, but don't know how to get there, follow your nose," he said cheerfully. His nose led him to a strange looking contraption propped against a signpost.

"May I borrow your little iron horse?" he asked the signpost.

Jonathin Spindle had just the right sort of legs for riding a bicycle that had no pedals, long and thin and very strong.

11

"When you know where you are going and you want to get there quicker, borrow an iron horse" he said.

He tied the paper bag holding his bread and cheese to the handlebars and got onto the contraption which was really an iron hobby-horse. His long feet pushed hard at the ground and the iron wheels fairly whizzed along. Bumpety, bumpety, bump.

"I'm off to see the world" he sang, as he sped along the lane and into the wood. "This must be the great forest where the monkeys, the elephants and the parrots live."

"What a large animal an elephant is to be sure," he gasped as a little brown rabbit hopped across the road in front of him, jumpety, jumpety, jump.

He watched the rabbit scurry down a burrow.

"So . . ." he said, with wonder in his voice, "Elephants live under the ground in tunnels."

The wood was only a small wood and Jonathin's legs moved very fast as they scudded along the ground, scrapety, scrapety, scrape. Flappety, flappety, flap.

He was thinking about the elephant he thought he had seen and he quite forgot to steer round the next corner he came to. Bumpety, bumpety, bump, he went, right across a freshly ploughed field.

"This must be the desert," said Jonathin, as mud splattered his boots and leggings. "I don't suppose it has rained here for years and years and years. I wonder if I will see a camel."

A tiny brown bird flew up from the furrow in front of him.

"Upon my word . . . a flying camel," shouted Jonathin Spindle.

He craned his long neck and peered up into the sky so that he could see the flying camel better and ran straight into a hedge!

The tangle of branches stopped the hobby-horse and he fell off with a bumpety, bumpety, bump.

"What a prickly place the world is," he said, as he pulled a thorn from his long nose. "I wish it would look where it is going. Hasn't it got a nose of its own to follow?"

He decided that as he was already sitting on the ground he might as well eat his lunch. Where was the brown paper bag holding his bread and cheese? It was high in the hedge, held there by the brambles and prickles.

"I suppose hedges get hungry too," he said, "But it might have asked first. Please fold up the bag and put it away tidily when you have finished eating," he called.

Jonathin remounted his little iron horse and carried on following his long nose. It led him to a duck pond.

14

THE LITTLE TRUCK THAT MADE THE TOWN JUMP

Dinky was a little truck who worked for Sam Jones, the builder, and he was very unhappy. Every day for weeks he had been doing the same journey — carrying bricks and sand and cement and pipes and timber to where Sam Jones and his men were building a new school.

Dinky liked working for Sam Jones, who was a big, jolly man with a loud, friendly voice. Dinky loved rushing to and from Sam Jones's builder's yard with the things the men wanted for building. He didn't even mind doing the same journey there and back every day. The trouble was that on this journey to the new school he had to go so slowly. In fact, he almost had to crawl.

Dinky was a smart truck. He was painted blue with yellow stripes, and all his metalwork gleamed like silver and sparkled in the sunlight. And he could go really fast.

He was the fastest of all Sam Jones's trucks and vans, and he loved speeding along the road, humming merrily, and when he carried a loose load he had great fun listening to it going *bumpety-bump-thud-bumpety-bump-thud* behind him, just as if it was beating time to the music of his engine!

But there was no fun at all on this slow journey to the new

school, for there was a big, rude truck that went along the
road at the same time as he did every day, and it stayed right
in front of him, in the middle of the road, and wouldn't let
him pass.

Once, Dinky tried to rush past the big truck, thinking it
would move to one side of the road; but it didn't. Dinky's

brakes had to go on sharply or he would have had to swerve on to the grass and he might have ended up in the ditch alongside.

After that, Dinky just had to rumble slowly along behind the big truck. He was most unhappy about it.

Then one day an astonishing thing happened. On being driven out of the shed where all Sam Jones's vans and trucks were kept, Dinky was loaded up with something big and heavy that he'd never seen before. It wasn't a boiler or a concrete mixer or a kitchen range. He couldn't see it very well, and he didn't know what it was. Dinky hurried out on to the road, but just as he began to get up speed, there, just in front of him, loomed up the big, rude truck.

"Honk, honk! Toot, toot!" Dinky's hooter blared out, but the big, rude truck took no notice; he just rumbled on, taking up most of the road and giving Dinky no room at all to pass.

Dinky was so eager to go faster that he gave a jerky kind of leap forward. The jerk broke the rope that kept the thing behind firmly tied up, and a sudden loud noise clanged out behind. It was so loud that Dinky jumped, and the big, rude truck jumped; the whole town jumped. CLANG, CLANG, CLANG!

"My word!" cried Sam Jones. "The school bell's broken loose!"

Then Dinky knew what it was he was carrying behind. It was a great big bell for the new school! It made a tremendous noise, and once it started clanging it kept on! CLANG, CLANG, CLANG!

The big, rude truck was so startled that it swung across
the road, bumped into a lamp-post and came to a sudden
stop.

Dinky rushed past. All the people on the pavements stopped
to stare as he rushed on with the bell clanging loudly behind
him. They thought he was a fire-engine! Shopkeepers hurried
out of their shops to see what was happening. Dogs barked.
Children shouted and cheered, and a policeman on point
duty held up all the traffic. CLANG, CLANG, CLANG!

Dinky had never enjoyed anything so much in his life. He
was excited "I'm a fire-engine!" he shouted, and raced on with
the bell clanging out behind him. What a noise it made!
People put their fingers in their ears so that they would not
hear it. And it didn't stop clanging till Dinky came to the
place where the new school was nearly built.

Sam Jones told all the men building the school what had happened, and he laughed and laughed, and they laughed and laughed, and everybody was pleased about it, though nobody quite so much as Dinky. He'd had a wonderful morning. He'd taught the big, rude truck a lesson and he'd made the whole town jump!

THE TALE OF THE TURNIP

One day, Grandpa Brown planted a turnip seed in a corner of his vegetable patch. He watered it, and pulled the weeds from around it, and it grew bigger and bigger and BIGGER.

When it was as big round, as his wife's tape measure was long, and that was very big round indeed, Grandpa Brown said,

"Wife, I fancy turnip broth for my dinner today. I will pull the turnip. When it is cooked we will have a feast fit for a king." He went to the vegetable patch and took hold of the turnip's green leaves, which by now reached almost as high as his chin, and pulled. And then he pulled a bit harder. Nothing happened. The turnip was stuck tight in the ground.

"Wife!" he called. "Please come and help me."

"Why are you taking so long?" asked Grandma Brown.

"Do not waste your breath talking wife, just put your arms round my waist, and when I say pull, pull."

"Yes husband," said Grandma Brown.

"Pull!" said Grandpa Brown. Grandpa Brown AND Grandma Brown pulled and pulled. Still the turnip did not move.

"Grandson!" called Grandma Brown. "Please come and help us."

"Fancy not being strong enough to pull a turnip from the ground," said the boy trying not to laugh.

"Do not waste breath laughing," said Grandma Brown. "Put your arms round my waist and when Grandpa says pull, pull."

"Pull!" said Grandpa Brown. Grandpa Brown, Grandma Brown, AND the boy, pulled and pulled. Still the turnip would not move.

24

"Sister!" called the boy. "Please come and help us."

"I am hungry, when will the broth be ready?" asked the girl.

"Do not waste breath talking," said the boy. "Put your arms round my waist and when Grandpa says pull, pull."

"Pull!" said Grandpa Brown. Grandpa Brown, Grandma Brown, the boy AND the girl, pulled and pulled. It really was a very stubborn turnip.

"Dog!" called the girl. "Please come and help us."

"Woof!" said the dog.

"Do not waste breath barking," said the girl. "When Grandpa says pull, pull."

"Pull!" said Grandpa Brown. Grandpa Brown, Grandma Brown, the boy, the girl AND the dog, pulled and pulled and PULLED. But it was all wasted effort. The turnip stuck in the ground as fast as glue sticks in a gluepot.

"Cat!" called the dog. "Please come and help us."

"Miaow!" said the cat.

"Do not waste breath miaowing," said the dog. "When Grandpa says pull, pull."

"Pull!" said Grandpa Brown. Grandpa Brown, Grandma Brown, the boy, the girl, the dog AND the cat pulled as hard as they possibly could. The turnip roots pulled even harder.

It really was the stubbornest turnip any of them had ever seen.

"We might as well give up," said Grandpa Brown sadly. "We cannot pull the turnip and we will never have our turnip broth."

"What a pity," sighed Grandma Brown. "I was quite

looking forward to making it."

"And I was looking forward to eating it," sighed the boy,
the girl, the dog, and the cat, one after the other.

"Let me help," squeaked a voice at their feet. It was a
mouse who had come from his hole to see what all the sighing
was about.

27

Grandpa Brown shook his head sadly. "The tiny amount of help you can give will make no difference at all," he said.

"At least let him try," said Grandma Brown, the boy, the girl, the dog, and the cat, all at the same time.

And so once again Grandpa Brown said, "Pull!" and once again Grandpa Brown, Grandma Brown, the boy, the girl, the dog, the cat, and this time the mouse as well, pulled . . . and PULLED . . .

And then, so suddenly, that they were all taken by surprise, the turnip came up from the ground in a shower of soil and tiny pebbles and they all fell backwards one on top of the other, with the turnip on top of them all.

When the broth was finally made, there was a special helping in a special dish for the mouse, for without his help there would have been no turnip broth at all.

SLIBBERSLOB THE GNOME

Slibberslob lived with Esmeralda in a bird-box at the bottom of Mrs. Sherbert's garden. He was a mischievous gnome. Esmeralda was always having to get him out of some trouble into which he had fallen. When she put on her witch hat, Esmeralda could do magic, which helped.

One morning, Esmeralda climbed down the ladder of twigs that led from the bird-box to the ground. She told Slibberslob that she was going to buy some balloons for his birthday party next week.

Slibberslob waved goodbye to her from the door of the bird-box. "Don't forget to dry the dishes and put them away," called Esmeralda, "and mind you empty the washing-up water down the drain."

"I'll leave the dishes to dry themselves," said Slibberslob to himself gleefully, "and Esmeralda can put them away when she gets back. I'm not climbing all the way down to the ground either, just to get rid of the washing-up water. It's easier to throw it out."

So instead of carrying the washing-up bowl carefully down to the ground, as Esmeralda always did, the naughty gnome picked up the bowl and flung the dirty water all over the roses growing below.

One of the roses broke off under the weight of the water, but, even worse, the stream of water swept all over a baby crow who was pecking insects from the roses.

"Caw, caw!" croaked the poor little crow, who was soaked with the water. He hadn't a single dry feather left on his body. Slibberslob held his sides and shook with laughter.

He thought the little wet crow looked very funny. The little baby crow flew off, croaking dismally, Slibberslob climbed down the twig-ladder and hurried over to the stone bowl in which Mrs. Sherbert put water for the birds to drink. "I'll have a swim," he chuckled. "Hey, you birds, shoo! Hop it! Fly away! You can have a drink when I've finished my bath — if there's any water left!" He scared the birds away and was soon splashing gaily about in the bowl — but not for long.

All of a sudden he saw a black shadow over the water and next instant he found himself caught up in a big beak and carried swiftly up in the air. "Wow!" he yelled. "Hey, put me down! What's happening? Help!" What was happening was that Mother Crow was flying with him up to her nest at the top of a very tall tree. In the nest with two other small crows was the baby crow Slibberslob had soaked with the washing-up water. All the crow babies croaked in surprise when Mother Crow dropped Slibberslob in among them.

"Has the funny little man come to play with us?" asked one of the little crows. "No. I've brought him up here to teach him not to throw water over my children," said Mother Crow. "Let me out at once!" cried Slibberslob angrily, but Mother Crow took no notice. "I shall go and peck up some lunch for you now, children," she added, shaking a claw at Slibberslob. Then she flew away.

Whatever was Slibberslob to do? He peeped over the edge of the nest, but he knew he couldn't climb down from it. It was swaying in the wind too, quite dizzily. "Oh, my beard and whiskers!" he muttered. "I am in a fix. I wish I'd emptied the water now as Esmeralda told me." Then suddenly he saw something in the sky. It was red and round. Slowly it drifted nearer. "Why," cried Slibberslob, "it's a balloon!" Yes, it was a red balloon, with a blue basket underneath. Slibberslob guessed at once that it was one of the balloons Esmeralda had gone to buy for his birthday party. "Esmeralda has done her magic," he chuckled. "Hurray!"

As the balloon sailed by, Slibberslob climbed up on to the side of the nest and jumped into the little basket. "Ho, ho, ho, home we go!" he laughed, and soon he was sailing through the air. Slowly the balloon sank down towards Mrs. Sherbert's garden.

There, waiting for him, was Esmeralda with her witch hat on. "I might have known you'd get into mischief while I was away," she grumbled as he stepped from the basket. "I had to use magic to find you and rescue you." "Thank you, Esmeralda. Your magic was very good. I enjoyed riding in the balloon." He peered into her shopping basket. "Now, what have you brought for lunch? I'm hungry." "Lunch will be ready, Slibberslob," said Esmeralda, smiling sweetly, "as soon as you've put the dishes away."

"Oh, my goodness!" groaned Slibberslob. "Oh, fishes! Those dishes!"

A RUNNING RACE

It was Sunday morning. Mrs. Hedgehog was busy in her kitchen and the Hedgehog children were playing hide and seek in the garden.

"I'm just going to the field to look at my turnips," called Mr. Hedgehog who liked a walk on Sunday mornings. He was half way there when he met Mr. Hare, who was also out walking.

Mr. Hare was going to look at his cabbages.

"Good morning," said Mr. Hedgehog in his usual polite and friendly manner. "Nice morning for a walk, isn't it?"

Mr. Hare stuck his nose in the air. "What does someone with legs as short as yours know about walking?" he said scornfully.

Mr. Hedgehog didn't like other animals making fun of his short legs.

"My legs are every bit as good as yours," he said.

"Fiddle-de-dee!" scoffed Mr. Hare. "That's nonsense and you know it. Why, I can outrun you any day."

"We will put it to the test," said Mr. Hedgehog. "I will wager you a cabbage to a turnip that *I* can run faster than *you*."

"What a ridiculous little hedgehog you are," said Mr. Hare. "But if you will insist on making yourself look foolish why should I stop you. Shall we begin?"

"I haven't had my breakfast yet," said Mr. Hedgehog. "I can't run on an empty stomach. I'll meet you in the big field in half an hour. We will run our race along the furrows."

"Very well," said Mr. Hare and went to get some breakfast himself.

"Quick wife! Quick!" said Mr. Hedgehog when he got home. "Take off your apron and come with me."

Of course Mrs. Hedgehog, who was so like Mr. Hedgehog that they looked like two peas from the same pod, wanted to know what the fuss was about. When Mr. Hedgehog told her she said Mr. Hare was quite right, he was silly.

"No hedgehog can run faster than a hare," she said. Little did she know. Mr. Hedgehog had a plan and he needed her help. They reached the far end of the field, where the race was to be run, while Mr. Hare was still eating his breakfast.

"Hide in that furrow wife," said Mr. Hedgehog. "When you hear me call 'I am here already' bob up your head and wave."

Mrs. Hedgehog didn't understand *why* she should do such a thing, but she agreed to do it all the same. When Mr. Hare arrived Mr. Hedgehog was waiting at the opposite end of the field.

"I'm ready," said Mr. Hedgehog. "Are you?"

Mr. Hare sniffed. He would show this silly hedgehog a thing or two. "Of course I'm ready," he said.

Ready! Steady! GO!

37

THEY WERE OFF!

Mr. Hare lolloped along, not really bothering to hurry. The furrows were deep and he couldn't see Mr. Hedgehog but he knew he had nothing to worry about. The turnip was as good as his. *His* legs were made for running. Mr. Hedgehog's were not. He couldn't believe his ears when he got to the far end of the field and heard Mr. Hedgehog call "I am here already", or his eyes, when he saw a hedgehog head pop up from the furrow next to his. How was he to know that although he had heard *Mr.* Hedgehog, he was seeing *Mrs.* Hedgehog? 'I'll have to run faster on the way back,' he thought.

But just before he reached the end of the furrow Mr. Hedgehog popped up at the end of his furrow. And what was more, he wasn't even panting.

"It looks as though I have won," said Mr. Hedgehog.

How was Mr. Hare to know that Mr. Hedgehog had been crouching in the furrow and hadn't run at all?

"Let us race again," said Mr. Hare, convinced there had been a mistake. A hedgehog *cannot* run faster than a hare. Everyone knows that.

Mr. Hedgehog was only too glad to oblige.

Every time Mr. Hare reached the far edge of the field, Mr. Hedgehog called out "I am here already" and Mr. Hare would see *Mrs.* Hedgehog and think he was seeing *Mr.* Hedgehog. He ran backwards and forwards for hours and didn't win once. How could he?

Mr. Hedgehog had been too clever for him, and in the end he had to part with one of his cabbages. He never did understand how it had happened. Mrs. Hedgehog said that really Mr. Hedgehog had cheated. But Mr. Hedgehog said, "Mr. Hare should not have made fun of my short legs. I wanted to teach him a lesson. Perhaps in future he will think twice before he is rude to someone.

40

KING FERDI AND HIS DRAGON

King Ferdi was a kind and happy man. But he hadn't been very happy for some time. He was worried — worried about his pet dragon.

Her name was Dragonia. She was a gentle dragon and full of fun until she went off her food and became droopy. She drooped all over the place and could hardly lift her tail to wag a welcome to her master.

"What's the matter, Dragonia?" he said, rubbing a little soft spot behind her ear. "Tell Ferdi! . . . Why are you so poorly?" Dragonia put her head on his knee, rolled her eyes and gave a big sigh.

The king ordered special meals to be cooked for her. They were served on golden dishes, but Dragonia gave them one sniff and turned away. She was getting thinner every day. King Ferdi was at his wit's end!

He sent for clever doctors. They were afraid to come near

41

her.

"She won't eat you!" roared the king. But they weren't so sure and backed away. He sent for the zoo keepers, but they said: "We have no idea what is wrong, Your Majesty. You see, we don't keep dragons."

He sent for chemists to mix medicine. She shut her jaws — tight!

42

"What can I do!" wailed the king. "Take her for a walk," suggested the queen. "You keep her indoors too much." Ferdi looked up. "You really think so?" he asked. "Of course!" declared his wife. "Get on your horse and lead her along. It will do you both good." The king in his best hat, and Dragonia in jewelled collar, left the palace.

People poked their heads out of windows. "Fancy! There's

the king with his dragon!" They called the children in. "Here
comes a dragon!"

Ferdi rode on and out of town. He saw circus tents and led
Dragonia towards them. "Get that thing out of here!" a man
shouted. "We don't need more animals — can hardly feed
what we have!" The king said he was sorry. "My pet won't
eat. What do you give your animals?"

"Raw meat for the lions. Hay for horses and elephants.
Fish for the seals," answered the man. "Fish!" repeated the
king. "Would you sell me some fish?" The man said he could
have one to try. "Then you must go," he added. "I can't risk
any illness spreading from your poor creature." The king
agreed — too upset to be angry. Fish was brought but
Dragonia wouldn't touch it. "Could I have a handful of hay?"
asked Ferdi. Hay was brought but again Dragonia refused.
"Raw meat, now I suppose?" said the circus man rudely.
"Yes, please!" said Ferdi politely. But it was useless.
Dragonia turned away. The king paid the man and left. When
they came to a green shady bank Ferdi stopped to rest.
Dragonia flopped down. The horse went under the trees.
Soon, all three were asleep.

Presently an old woman passed leading her loaded donkey.
She had been to market but had sold nothing. A good smell
came from the bundles; Dragonia's nose twitched even as
she slept.

Suddenly, the dragon awoke, sniffing the air. Then she was up and following the smell. Hearing shuffling steps, the old woman turned.

"Why, you poor dear!" she cried. "YOU'RE STARVING!" She pulled carrots from the donkey's load and immediately the dragon took a nibble. "That's right, my dear," said the old woman, "slowly now — you'll have a pain if you gobble." Dragonia ate one carrot, then another — and another. The old woman took more from her sack and still Dragonia went on feeding. "I'd like to meet your master!" declared the old woman. "Someone rich by the look of your collar . . . I'd report him to the king!"

When Ferdi awoke he moaned aloud: "Oh dear! Where's my Dragonia?" He searched around: then looked down the road. There sat his dear dragon — gazing at a little old woman and eating! . . . EATING!! "That's enough my dear," she said. "You come along home with me, now. I'm glad I didn't sell my carrots, after all!"

"So am I, madam!" said the king from behind her. The old woman was amazed. "You!" she exclaimed. "King Ferdi! . . . You should be ashamed! Didn't you know your dragon needed carrots?"

The king explained: "We never see raw carrots at the palace!" She offered him one. "Try that, Your Majesty!" Ferdi scrunched — then smiled. "Delicious! How can I reward

45

you?" She shook her head. "I don't need reward, sir."

"Isn't there anything you'd like?" begged Ferdi. Just then his horse appeared. "Yes," she said. "I'd like to ride your beautiful horse and lead your darling dragon!" He laughed: "And so you shall!"

Helping her up he gave her Dragonia's lead. He led the donkey. They set off together and do you know — they were all eating carrots!

46

THE ENCHANTED KETTLE

Once upon a time there was a man in Ancient China who had a very fine kettle. It had a slender spout and a gracefully curved handle, and when it was filled with water and set on the fire, it bubbled merrily.

Or that is, it did . . . until one fine day . . .

The day began as every other day begins. It was a perfectly ordinary day until the old man decided to make himself a cup of tea. He lifted the kettle from its place beside the fire and set it among the flames, little knowing he was about to get the biggest surprise he had ever had in his life.

The kettle jumped from the fire. But that was not all it did, though that was enough to make the old man gasp. It grew four short legs, a hairy tail, and the striped head of a badger. It danced round and round the room until the old man grew dizzy from watching it. Then it drew in its head, its legs, and its tail, and stood absolutely still.

The old man could not be sure whether he was dreaming or not, but he decided to take no chances. He lifted the kettle by pushing a stick through the handle, he didn't dare touch the kettle himself, and dropped it into a wooden box. He tied

48

the lid down securely so that if the kettle decided it wanted
to dance again it would have to do it inside the box, and
stayed as far away from it as he could.

The next day a tinker happened to pass that way selling
kettles, and pots and pans and other things. Here was a
chance to get rid of the kettle. The old man called to the
tinker.

"I have a beautiful kettle which is no use to me. Would
you like to buy it?"

A tinker is always willing to do business. He bought the
kettle for just a few pence and put it into his sack.

"You have a real bargain there," said the old man.

"I'm sure I have," said the tinker. Who of course did not
know how unusual the kettle was. And you may be sure the
old man did not tell him. He was rather pleased with himself
for getting rid of the mysterious kettle so easily.

That night as the tinker lay in bed he heard a strange
noise coming from the sack and went to investigate. Out
jumped the kettle, with four short legs, a hairy tail and a
striped badger's head growing from its rounded sides. It
raced round and round the room in a mad and merry dance.

Now the tinker was a man who was untroubled by anything strange or unusual. Instead of being frightened, he sat on the edge of his bed and laughed and laughed at the kettle's antics.

"I will teach it some tricks," he said. "If it makes me laugh I am sure it will make others laugh too."

The tinker was absolutely right. Everyone especially the

50

children, laughed until they cried at the things the badger kettle did. The tinker travelled far and wide, from market place to market place, and everywhere he went people said,

"Hooray, here comes the tinker with the enchanted kettle. What new tricks will we see today?"

Before very long news of the wonderful kettle reached the palace and one day a royal messenger came to the tinker.

"His Majesty wishes to see the enchanted kettle. You are hereby summoned to bring it to the palace."

No one dares to disobey an Emperor's command, least of all a humble tinker and he went straight to the palace that very day. He had never been inside a palace before. He was amazed at what he saw. But nowhere near as amazed as the Emperor when he saw what the kettle could do. The Emperor and his courtiers laughed as loudly and as long at its antics as the people in the market place had done.

"It is good to laugh so much," said the Emperor. "You must bring your kettle to see me again." And because the kettle had put him in a good mood he gave the tinker a bag of gold.

The enchanted kettle made a fortune for the tinker, and he really grew very fond of it, but he found himself thinking more and more of the old man who had sold it to him.

"I must not be greedy," he said. "The kettle has made a fortune for me, I must let it make a fortune for the old man." And although it made him very sad to part with the badger kettle he took it back to the old man.

"Goodbye little friend," he said, as he gently patted its rounded sides, "I shall miss you."

The old man was very pleased to have the kettle back, for of course, he too had heard of its fame. He rapped it sharply on its lid and said:

"Grow your four legs, your hairy tail and your striped badger's head and dance for me."

But the kettle, who if the truth be known, was just a little tired of doing tricks, refused to obey the old man's command. And although the old man spent many hours watching it boil away on the fire, hoping to see it jump from the flames and dance round the room, it never did.

It made beautiful, fragrant cups of tea, but from that day on, it behaved like any other respectable kettle.

THE MAGIC POT

Once upon a time, there was a girl who lived with her mother in a tiny house on the outskirts of a small town. They were very poor and sometimes they were very hungry. They often had nothing to eat at all.

54

One day, when the girl was out in the woods searching for mushrooms and blackberries, she met an old woman who was carrying an empty iron pot.

"Take it," said the old woman putting the pot into her hands. "When you are hungry, say to it 'Little pot boil'. When you have enough, say, 'Little pot stop'."

The girl thought it very strange, but she took the pot home and told her mother what the old woman had said.

"Put it on the table, say the words, and we will see what happens," said her mother.

"Little pot boil," said the girl. Hardly were the words spoken than the pot began to bubble and hiss, and steam began to rise from it.

"It's filling up," gasped the girl.

"It's truly a magic pot," said her mother. "Stop it before it overflows."

"Little pot stop," said the girl. The bubbling and hissing stopped at once. "What a delicious smell," said the girl.

"That looks and smells very like porridge to me," said her mother. "Bring two plates and two spoons and we will taste it".

It was the sweetest, creamiest, nicest porridge either of them had ever tasted. And with a magic porridge pot like that at their command, their days of being hungry were over. It didn't matter how much porridge they ate, there was always some more to be had at the command 'Little pot boil'.

One day, when the girl was out, her mother set the pot on the table, and said,

56

"Little pot boil". The bubbling began, the steam began to rise, the delicious smell of porridge began to fill the room. The sweet creamy porridge reached the brim of the pot. The girl's mother opened her mouth to say the words to stop it and found she couldn't remember them. All she could think to say, was, "Um er . . . that's enough". A tiny trickle of porridge began to run down the OUTSIDE of the porridge pot. The pot had never done that before. "Stop . . . stop . . . " she shouted in a panic. "I don't want any more . . . stop filling up . . . go away . . . " The harder she tried to remember the right words the worse it became.

The pot bubbled and bubbled. The trickle of porridge became a stream. It spread across the table and fell in a sticky cascade to the floor.

"Whatever shall I do?" she wailed as she climbed onto a chair. "Please . . . please . . . please stop . . . please pot! . . . "

The pool of porridge spread to the door and ran out into the street.

"Stop! . . Stop! . . " she shouted. "Come back porridge . . . get back into the pot . . . please stop! . . " The porridge pot took no notice. It would only stop when it was given the right command. But what WAS the right command?

The sweet creamy porridge began to behave like an overflowing river. It ran on and on along the streets, into the houses and the dog kennels. It filled up the fish ponds and the drains.

"What's happening?" shouted the citizens of the town as they took off their shoes and waded through the sticky mess.

58

"It's the pot . . . it won't stop," cried the girl's mother.

The citizens began to shout commands then. The dogs began to bark and the cats began to miaow.

"Stop making porridge before we all drown . . . Stop! . . Stop! . ."

The girl was visiting at the far edge of the town. She heard the commotion and looked out of the window to see what the noise was about. As soon as she saw the rivers of porridge oozing through the streets she guessed at once what had happened. She ran home as fast as the sticky porridge would let her.

"Do something, do something quickly!" urged the townsfolk. When she got home her mother was still shouting commands at the pot. "Stop cooking . . . stop bubbling . . . Stop! . . Stop! . ."

"Little pot stop." said the girl. THAT was the right command and the pot DID stop. Instantly.

"I'll only use the pot when you are here in future," said her mother. "I don't want that to happen again."

Neither did anyone else. It took simply ages to clean up the town and no one wants to do that kind of sticky job twice.

THUMBLING

Once upon a time, there was a man who had a son no bigger than his thumb. He called him Thumbling and taught him how to cut and sew cloth, and how to look after himself, and not get caught by the cat or fall down a mouse-hole. Though he was so tiny, Thumbling was as brave and as bold as any other boy and just as mischievous. He had many adventures.

One day, Thumbling said to his father,

"Father, I want to see something of the world."

"And so you shall my son," said Thumbling's father. He knew Thumbling would only sigh loudly and sew big uneven stitches until he had his way. The sooner he went and saw the world, the sooner he would come back home and help with the sewing.

61

He made Thumbling a sword from a darning needle and a
knob of red wax and he made him a belt from button thread
so that he could buckle the sword round his waist.

Thumbling's mother was cooking at the fireplace.

"That smells good," said Thumbling. "I'll have some of

that before I go." He leant over the pot to sniff the delicious aroma of cooking lentils.

"Come back at once and say goodbye properly," grumbled his mother, as the steam from the cooking pot picked Thumbling up and wafted him up the chimney.

"Bye . . ." called Thumbling as he sailed away like a feather, "This is the only way to travel."

He finally sank to the ground on the far side of the valley. He found work with a man who was a tailor like his father. For a while Thumbling behaved himself, but he began to miss his mother's cooking. The tailor's wife was always forgetting to put the meat in the cooking pot and was always boiling the potatoes dry.

"One day," he said, teasingly, "I shall go away if you don't feed me better and before I do, I will write on your door, 'Too many burnt potatoes and not enough meat'."

The tailor's wife was very cross. After all, she always did her best. She couldn't help it if the cooking went wrong sometimes.

"You little . . . grasshopper," she snapped and she picked up the dishcloth and tried to hit him with it.

"Ho . . ho . . can't catch me!" teased Thumbling, dodging out of the way with the greatest of ease. It is easy to dodge when you are small and easy to hide under a thimble.

"Here I am," he called, to make sure she was looking his way, and when he saw that she was, he poked out his tongue.

"You naughty little grasshopper . . ." she scolded as she lifted the thimble, "But I've caught you now."

"Oh no, you haven't," laughed Thumbling and he ran along the folds in the tablecloth playing hide and seek with her.

The tailor's wife caught hold of the corner of the cloth and pulled it to the floor. What a noise there was as the plates crashed and the knives clattered.

"Can't catch me!" sang Thumbling and jumped down into a crack in the table. He unbuckled his darning needle sword and every time the tailor's wife moved her hand towards him he pricked her thumb with it.

'I'll get you out of there," she scolded.

While she went to look for something to prise him out of the crack, Thumbling climbed into the table drawer.

"Yoo hoo, I'm here . . . " he called through the keyhole.

"Then I've caught you at last!" said the tailor's wife.

"Oh no, you haven't!" shouted Thumbling as she pulled the drawer open. He leapt onto her hand and flourished his darning needle sword.

"Ow!" shrieked the tailor's wife, and the drawer fell to the floor and scattered its contents far and wide. Thumbling decided the time had come for him to see some more of the world.

"Bye!" he called as he hopped, skipped and jumped along the path. "I'll leave you to clear away the mess."

"Away with you!" shouted the tailor's wife. "I would rather have a hive full of bees in my house than you." And with that she slammed the door and Thumbling went on his way.

66

RIMSKI AND THE WEATHER-VANE

Rimski was a young rooster. He had golden feathers round his neck, tail feathers of shining green and a croaky voice which grew stronger every day. Each morning very early, he flapped up on to the yard gate. There he stretched his neck and his wings trying out his 'Cock-a-doodle-doo!' . . . Yes, it was improving — reaching a high note.

After he had crowed, he stopped to listen, hoping someone would answer him. One morning from a long way away came a faint 'Cock-a-doodle-doo!' That was a great day for Rimski. He strutted about feeling very proud.

One day, as he made his first crow, the church clock chimed. He hadn't noticed it before — it had just been mended. The sound annoyed him. It spoilt his own wonderful sound. Lifting his head to see where the strange sound had come from, he saw something shining at the top of the church spire. Then he looked again — and again! Was it possible?

A bird up there? . . . Yes, a golden one! . . What did it mean by singing out that silly 'Ding-dong, ding-dong' rubbish! Why couldn't it give a proper 'Cock-a-doodle-doo!'? This was serious. The matter needed his careful attention.

Pulling himself up tall, Rimski let out a loud and long 'Cock-a-doodle-doo!' He gave his feathers a shake, as if to say, "That should fix him!" . . . There was no answer. "Ha!" said Rimski, "He can't beat that!"

Later, the chimes went again, to be followed by 'Dong, dong, dong, dong, dongngng!' Rimski was very angry. It bothered him. What could he do? He couldn't sleep that night and through the hours he heard its chimes and its dongs. By morning he had made up his mind.

He'd go and see him — this 'Ding-dong Goldie' as he had
nicknamed him. HE would make him change his tune!

Up on the gate, then out into the lane — Rimski strutted
off. Mrs. Tabby Cat saw him as she sat washing herself.

"Good morning!" she called, "Going somewhere?"

"Of course!" answered Rimski. "I have important business
to attend to. That bird up there — I'm going to put him in his
place!" He tossed his head towards the church spire. Mrs.
Tabby glanced up: "That IS his place!" she said . . . Rimski
ignored her. Presently he came to a donkey, tethered on the
grass.

"Hee-haw!" cried the donkey. "Could you please undo this
rope? . . . I'd love to come for a walk!" Rimski didn't even
stop. "Sorry! I'm off to teach that bird a lesson!" . . . "Which
bird?" asked the donkey. Once again Rimski tossed his head
towards the church. "Oh, he only does what the wind tells
him," said the donkey. "He'll do what I tell him!" boasted
Rimski.

In the churchyard, he perched on a stone to give a loud
'Cock-a-doodle-doo!' No one answered.

Mrs. Blackbird came, searching for worms, then stopped
to chat. Rimski explained why he had come; but she found it
puzzling that he should want to quarrel with the weather-
vane!

69

When the clock chimed again, Rimski was furious. "There, listen! I'll stop him — this weather-vane!" Mrs. Blackbird said he would have to go up because weather-vanes never came down. "How?" he asked. "You could fly," she suggested. But Rimski made excuses so she took him to the steps. Up and up! Round and round! "Keep going!" she called. His head spun!

At last he came to a wide platform. The clock whirred — then blared out. Poor Rimski! It was terrifying! He found the

workman's ladder fixed to the spire. Holding with his beak, he went up slowly. There was the bird. Golden? Yes: but no bird — just a metal shape. It swung round flinging Rimski off — far out into space.

He flapped and flapped! The ground looked miles away — then nearer and nearer! He was going to crash! A strong

71

wind lifted him just in time. As it was, he flopped down —
pitching on to his nose.

Mrs. Blackbird cheered him up. "What a flight, sir! You'll
be famous!" Rimski felt better. "Thank you, madam. I can
certainly tell the world about Goldie up there. He's not real
— only a painted thing going round and round!" Mrs.
Blackbird laughed. "Whichever way the wind blows, I
suppose. HE can't make the sounds then! Could they come
from the clock, d'you think!" Rimski considered. "Possibly!..
Possibly! Yes, you can take it from me — they came from
the clock." Mrs. Blackbird went on, "If we counted each dong
would that tell us the time?" Rimski tried to think. He
couldn't keep up with this clever blackbird. The clock struck.
"Gracious!" she cried, "I must be off! Goodbye!" Rimski
stared after her, gave himself a shake-and started for home.

The donkey asked how he'd got on. "Fine!" said Rimski.
"That bird is just a weather-vane turning in the wind!" The
donkey laughed.

Mrs. Tabby Cat opened one eye. "Anything exciting
happen?" she asked. "Of course!" he replied. "I climbed the
spire, checked the clock and the weather-vane, then flew
down." Tabby grinned. "Well! There's something to crow
about!"... He flapped on to his gate. The cat's right! he
thought. Stretching up, Rimski gave his very best
'Cock-a-doodle-doo!'

SAMMY SCARECROW'S PARTY

For year after year Sammy Scarecrow had stood in Farmer Green's field forgotten. His clothes had become old and tattered, and his hat was full of holes. Then one evening, the Wood Wizard stepped out of the wood and said: "Sammy, tomorrow is your twenty-first birthday, and the woodland folk have decided to give a party for you. The birds and the bees have promised to take the invitations out. The party will begin at sunset, so stay awake, Sammy."

Sammy had never been so excited. He didn't know what to do with himself all next day. At sunset the Wood Wizard stepped out of the wood again. He handed Sammy a little box. "Many happy returns of your twenty-first birthday, Sammy."

Eagerly Sammy opened the box. Inside was a tiny acorn, and underneath it was written:—

Plant me in a moonbeam's glow;
Water me to make me grow.

Before the moon rose, the guests began to arrive. The Elfin Folk flew in on the backs of moths. Leprechauns galloped in on Irish jaunting carts. They wore green suits with feathers in their hats. The Fairy Queen came in grand style in a coach drawn by a long team of ants, with ladybirds as footmen. Dwarfs rode in on the backs of moles from underground tunnels.

73

Kelpies arrived on tiny horses, and a party of gnomes marched in singing and playing musical instruments.

All the guests brought presents. Sammy was thrilled when he found among them a new red overcoat for the winter, a pair of baggy blue trousers, a yellow scarf, and a shiny top

hat for his head. "Thank you, thank you!" he cried, "I do wish I had a feast for our guests."

"It's time you planted your acorn," the Wood Wizard said. "Look! The moon has risen."

Carefully Sammy planted the acorn in the path of a

75

moonbeam, and watered it. In moments it became a great oak-tree.

Sammy cried out in delight. The Wood Wizard, wearing his tall pointed hat, stepped to the tree, stretched out his hand towards it, and called out in a loud voice:—

"Birthday tree, to be of use
Show the guests what you produce."

At once things began to appear on the tree, on twigs and branches and leaves — fudge, candies, liquorice, jellies of different colours, ice-creams, dewdrop drinks, cakes, cookies, tasty titbits of all kinds.

Sammy cried out delightedly: "Please help yourselves!" The guests did help themselves; but whatever they took from the tree was at once replaced by another ice-cream or cake or whatever it was. The Wood Wizard cried:—

"Now feast all night and dance with glee
Round Sammy Scarecrow's birthday tree!"

Dance and feast the guests did, until at last the Wood Wizard held up his hand and cried:—

"Midnight is about to strike.
Candles, candles, come alight!"

There was a flash, and twenty-one candles lit up on the tree. Everyone cheered and clapped. Linking hands, all the guests danced round the tree, singing "Happy birthday to you, happy birthday to you, happy birthday, dear Sammy, happy birthday to you!"

They danced and sang and feasted until somewhere a clock struck twelve — midnight. The candles went out. The tree shrank into the ground. The guests whispered goodnight to Sammy and stole away. Soon all was silent.

"Thank you, Wood Wizard!" cried Sammy, "Thank you, all! I'll never, never forget this wonderful party."

Well, if ever you see a scarecrow in a field wearing a red overcoat, baggy blue trousers, a yellow scarf, and a top hat set at a jaunty angle on his head, you'll know it's Sammy Scarecrow, and YOU will remember his wonderful twenty-first birthday party, won't you?

THE SULTAN'S PROBLEM

Once upon a time, in a land where the sun is always hot and the people wear loose flowing robes and turbans, there was a Sultan with a problem. In the streets the people were saying,

"What is the Sultan doing with the money we pay him in taxes? Is he keeping it for himself?"

And in the palace the Sultan was saying, "Why are my
people grumbling? Why have they stopped paying their
taxes?"

"Your people ARE paying taxes," whispered the Wise Man,
"But your Tax Collector is putting the money into his own
pocket."

The Sultan was very angry.

"Find me a new Tax Collector immediately." he said.

The Sultan tried one tax collector after another and still the money disappeared. The people began to mutter angrily,

"The Sultan is stealing the money we pay in taxes instead of using it to build schools and hospitals. Down with the Sultan!"

The Sultan was desperate. He summoned the Wise Man. "What shall I do?" he asked.

The Wise Man sat and thought for three days. On the afternoon of the third day he came to the Sultan and said,

"Make an announcement that you are looking for a new Tax Collector and leave the rest to me."

Early next morning the announcement was made, and by afternoon the antechamber was full. There were fat men wearing flowing robes, thin men wearing flowing robes. Men wearing embroidered robes. Men wearing robes of rich silk and brocade. And one man wearing a robe that was plain and threadbare. The rich men in their rich robes pointed at him and laughed. What was such a poor man doing applying for such a responsible post? He was just wasting his time. The Sultan would have more sense than to appoint a poor man as his Tax Collector. At last the Wise Man, who had been busy elsewhere, came into the antechamber.

"The Sultan will see you all together," he said. "STOP!" he ordered, as the richly robed and turbaned men rushed towards the door, all anxious to be the first one through, "You must leave the room one at a time. The corridor leading to the Sultan's apartment is narrow. There is room for only one of you to pass along it at a time." The Wise Man would not let anyone into the corridor until the man in front had reached the far end.

The corridor was long and very dark. Something seemed to have happened to the lamps that usually glimmered along its walls. One after another the men stumbled along, reaching and feeling with their hands as they went.

At last everyone was assembled before the Sultan.

"What do I do now?" whispered the Sultan. He was relying on the wisdom of the Wise Man.

"Order everyone to Dance," whispered the Wise Man.

"Dance?" whispered the Sultan. He couldn't keep the surprise from his voice.

"Yes," said the Wise Man. So the Sultan clapped his hands and ordered the dancing to begin, though he hadn't the remotest idea what dancing had to do with tax collecting.

After a few moments he turned to the Wise Man and said,

"I don't understand. I have never seen so many clumsy dancers in my life. What is wrong with them all? They look as though they have feet made of lead."

"Not that man," said the Wise Man, pointing to the man
whose flowing robes were clean, but plain and threadbare.
He was swirling and dancing as though HIS feet were made
of thistle-down.

"Stop the dancing," said the Wise Man. All the dancers, except one, sank thankfully to the floor and mopped their perspiring brows. The Wise Man called the Poor Man to his side.

"Have every man's robes searched," said the Wise Man.
"Why do that?" whispered the Sultan.
"Because," said the Wise Man, "The darkened corridor
through which every man had to pass alone, was piled with
golden coins and precious stones."

Now the Sultan understood. No one can dance and spring
in the air like thistle-down if his pockets are weighed down
with stolen jewels.

There was but one man whose pockets were empty, and
that was the man standing beside the Wise Man. The
Sultan had found an honest man. He made him Collector of
Taxes, and peace was restored to the land.

TAKING A DONKEY TO MARKET

Once upon a time, there was an old man who had a donkey he wanted to sell. One fine day, when the field had been weeded, the chickens fed and the house dusted, he and his son, and the donkey of course, set off for market.

The way to market was along a winding country road. It was hot, and the old man did not feel like walking.

"We might as well make use of the donkey while we still have him," he said. He tied a knot in the four corners of his red kerchief and put it on his head to protect it from the sun and climbed onto the donkey's back. Young John took hold of the halter round the donkey's neck and they set off at a steady pace, neither hurrying nor idling, but gently jog, jog, jogging along.

The old man was gazing upwards at a soaring skylark, when he heard someone shout,

"Shame on you old man for riding when your son is walking."

The old man blushed and looked ashamed. He slid from the donkey's back and took the halter from his son's hand.

"You ride a while, and let me lead the donkey," he said.

They had settled down to a steady jog, jog, jog, again when they met some women returning from market with laden baskets.

"Shame on you," they cried, shaking their fists at Young John. "A young man like you riding when your old father is walking." John's face went as red as his father's had done.

"The women are right Father," he said, "I shouldn't be riding when you are walking."

"Why don't we both ride?" said the old man.

"Now that is what I call a good idea," said Young John and taking his father's hand, he pulled him up behind him.

"What a pleasant day it is to be sure," said the old man, as they jog, jog, jogged along, listening to the skylarks and sniffing the sweet scent of hedgerow flowers. "I could jog along like this for ever."

But their peaceful ride was soon to be interrupted.

"Shame on you!" shouted some men who were making hay in a nearby field. "Shame on you!"

"Why . . . what have we done?" asked the old man in bewilderment.

"Two grown men riding on a little donkey . . . How can you be so cruel, and his head not even protected from the sun."

The old man and his son blushed as red as the scarlet poppies growing in the field. They quickly slid from the donkey's back.

"They are absolutely right," said Young John, "We shouldn't both be riding on the donkey."

"What shall we do?" asked the old man, taking the knotted kerchief from his own head and placing it between the

donkey's ears. "If I ride people will say I should let you ride, if YOU ride people will say you should let me ride. If we BOTH ride that will be wrong too. What shall we do? How can we please everyone we meet?"

The donkey stood and waited. He was patient. He didn't mind waiting while they made up their minds, it gave him time to nibble at the grass.

"I know what we can do," said Young John at last, "Instead of letting the donkey carry us, WE can carry the donkey."

"Now why didn't I think of that myself," said the old man. "No one can possibly complain about that arrangement."

The donkey didn't like being carried. No self-respecting donkey would. He brayed a bit, but he didn't struggle. He thought it best not to. He had no fancy to be dropped in the middle of the road.

The old man and his son saw no one else until they reached the market place. The donkey was very heavy and they were hot and tired by the time they got there, but of one thing they were sure, no one would call shame upon them now, or accuse them of ill-treating their donkey. No one did. Instead they were greeted with great shouts of laughter.

"Fancy carrying the donkey, when the donkey should be carrying you," shouted the people in a chorus.

"By trying to please everyone," sighed the old man, "We have pleased no one. In future we will please ourselves."

Which is what they should have done in the first place!

PIP THE PUP

Pip the Pup trotted out into the garden and sniffed the sweet morning air. He was feeling ready for anything. He looked this way and that way and behind him. And then he saw his tail. It stopped wagging as soon as he looked at it.

He looked at it with one eye for a time. He couldn't make up his mind whether it belonged to him or whether it was something that followed him about.

Pip was only a baby puppy, and there were lots of things he wasn't sure about. The tail was one of them.

The tail didn't move or make a sound. Pip gave a sharp bark at it to warn it that he had got his eye on it and it must not try any tricks on him.

Then he went on his way, growling loudly to show anybody who happened to be about that he was a dangerous fellow.

A sparrow hopped on to the lawn. Pip made a dash at it, but tripped and fell nose-first into a flower-bed. The sparrow went on hopping around just as if Pip wasn't there, so Pip barked furiously to show he wasn't a dog to be ignored.

Then he stopped and listened. Somebody was barking back! "Wuff, wuff, wuff!" barked Pip sharply. Then he cocked his head on one side and listened. "Wuff, wuff, wuff!"

He was right! Someone was answering him. Another dog! Off down the garden path dashed Pip, through the gate and into the lane. He just fancied a jolly romp with a dog friend. But which was the way to take?

Pip hesitated, not certain whether to go up or down the lane or over the meadow. Then he saw Harry the Horse trotting towards him down the lane.

"Excuse me," he said politely, "but do you know where another dog lives around here?"

"There are no dogs round here," snorted Harry. "You're the only dog, and you're not really a dog — yet. Good day!"

Harry splashed through a puddle in the lane and went on his way. Pip went thoughtfully over to the puddle and had a drink. Then he sat down in it and had a think.

Just then, Mrs. Penny Pig came bustling down the lane, followed by all her eight piglets, in single file.

"Oh, good morning, Mrs. Pig," said Pip. "Please can you tell me where another dog lives round here?"

"ANOTHER dog?" Mrs. Pig grunted, "What do you mean, ANOTHER dog? There aren't any dogs round here, and I hope there never will be.

But I suppose," she added, looking sharply at Pip with her beady eyes, "I suppose YOU will be a dog some day. Come along, piglets or we shall be late for market."

She hurried off, with her eight piglets squealing to each other behind her.

Pip scratched his ear. Then he thought it would be a good idea to scratch all over while he was about it. He felt much better after a thorough scratch. He gave a sharp bark. Ah, there it was again, a sharp bark in the distance, and not so far away, either!

"There!" cried Pip delightedly. "I wasn't mistaken. Wuff, wuff, wuff!"

"Wuff, wuff, wuff!" came the answering bark again.

Happily, Pip ran off up the lane, giving a sharp bark every now and again to let the other dog know he was coming. And the other dog barked back! At any moment now he would run into the other dog, thought Pip. He was so excited that he didn't really look where he was going, and instead of running into the other dog he ran right into a wall. It was a high wall and a hard wall. Pip backed away. He sat down and rubbed his nose with his paw. He looked up at the wall and barked at it thoughtfully. The other dog barked back, very loudly, just in front of him!

"Why," cried Pip, "the other dog's there, just on the other side of the wall. Wuff, wuff, wuff!"

At that moment, there was a rustling and a stirring high up in a tree close by. The enormous eyes of Mrs. Owl peered down at Pip. "Whatever is the meaning of this dreadful noise?" she scolded. "Don't you know I go to sleep during the day? How dare you make such a disturbance!"

"Oh, dear!" said Pip, "I'm very sorry, Mrs. Owl. I forgot you would be in bed. I was just saying hello to the other dog behind the wall." "Other dog? What other dog?" said Mrs. Owl. "There's no dog behind the wall, or in front of it, either," she added, peering down at the baby puppy, "because YOU can hardly be called a dog."

"There is a dog," said Pip, "Listen! You can hear him bark at me. Wuff, wuff, wuff!"

"Wuff, wuff, wuff!" came back to him. "There! Did you hear?" cried Pip. "You silly, stupid, noisy puppy!" cried Mrs. Owl crossly. "That is not another dog. It's YOU. It's your own bark coming back to you from the wall — an echo!" Oh, dear! Poor Pip was so disappointed he could have cried. But just as he was about to let a little tear fall, he heard a voice far down the lane. It was calling HIM. "Pip! Pip! Where are you, Pip? Come along! It's time to go and meet the children from school."

All Pip's troubles vanished. He shot down the lane as fast as he could go, slithering over muddy places and splashing through puddles, the other dog that wasn't a dog but only an echo quite forgotten. His little master and mistress, his very best playmates, were coming home from school!

A SINGING LESSON

Fred Frog had a deep baritone voice and he liked to sing.

"Please sing me a song Fred," Freda Frog would say. Fred would first find a place to sit and then he would wobble his chin and serenade her with the croakiest of croaks.

"Oh Fred, that is beautiful," Freda would say, her own voice full of admiration. Whereupon Fred would swell with pride and wobble his chin harder, and sing louder, and longer, and hardly stop to take breath at all. But though

Freda liked to hear Fred sing, there were those who thought
his voice sounded like a rusty old hinge on a broken-down
door.

One day, when Fred was singing, Reggie Reed-Warbler
called.

"Hey Fred, where's your oil can?"

"I should take some singing lessons if I were you," called Wally Wagtail.

"We can't hear OURSELVES sing with that racket going on," called the curlews.

"You sound like a cornflake with a sore throat," said the meadow-pipit.

The underneath part of Fred's chin stopped wobbling and his lip started to wobble instead. His feelings were hurt.

"Take no notice," said Freda. "They only say those things because they are jealous of your beautiful voice."

"Jealous of HIS voice," laughed the birds. "When we have such beautiful voices of our own? Don't be silly . . . now boys, let's show those frogs what real singing is all about."

The birds whistled and sang and filled the sky and the wind with the beautiful sounds that only birds can make. Poor Fred. A tear rolled down his cheek. He slid noiselessly into the water and hid in the mud on the bottom of the pond.

"Please don't cry," said Freda as she sidled into the mud beside him. "Your voice is the most beautiful voice in the world to me."

"If only I could sing like a bird," sighed Fred. "If only I could whistle and trill." And no matter what Freda said, Fred would not come out of the mud.

100

"Where's Fred?" asked Reggie Reed-Warbler next morning.

"You have hurt his feelings because you laughed at him," said Freda. "You have made him ashamed of his own voice and now he wishes he could sing like you."

Reggie Reed-Warbler thought for a moment. The birds hadn't meant to be unkind to Fred. "If he wants to sing like a bird, then we will teach him," he said. "Go and fetch him, Freda."

Freda really did prefer Fred's voice the way it was, but she went and got him all the same because she knew that was what Fred would have wanted. Fred came up and sat beside her on a lily pad and waited for his lesson to begin. The birds sat in the reeds facing him.

"This shouldn't take long," said Reggie.

Fred concentrated very hard. He really did. First Reggie showed him how to sing. Then Wally tried. And then all the other birds tried. Still Fred's voice did nothing but croak and creak and groan.

"No . . . no . . . Not like that," said Reggie for the hundredth time as yet another peculiar squeaky croak came from Fred's throat.

"I'm trying . . . I really am," said Fred.

"He is . . ." said Freda. "I can tell."

"You're being stubborn," shouted Reggie at last, "You don't want to sing like a bird."

"But I do . . . I do . . ." sobbed Fred. His poor green face looked back at him from the water. His tears plopped like pebbles and made his reflection disappear.

Tired and exasperated though the birds were, they began to feel sorry for him.

"Do cheer up," they said. "It's not your fault you can't sing like a bird."

It was then that Freda had an idea. "I don't suppose," she said, "that birds can croak like frogs either."

Fred's head jerked up and his tears stopped.

"Of course they can," said Reggie.

"Let's hear you then," said Freda.

The birds tried, they really did, but the sounds that came from their throats as they tried to croak like frogs were as strange as the sounds that came from Fred's throat when he tried to sing like a bird.

"I must admit," said Reggie, "that Fred is better at croaking than we are."

"I told you he had a beautiful voice," said Freda.

"I suppose he has, for a frog," admitted Reggie.

And that was how it ended, for after all, who wants to listen to a bird who croaks like a frog, or a frog who sings like a bird. A frog is a frog and a bird is a bird. Frogs croak, birds whistle, and that's the way it should be.

McTAVISH'S MOUSTACHE

McTavish was growing a curly black moustache. Mrs. McTavish didn't like it very much. Every morning she would say,

"Well, McTavish, are you going to shave off that silly moustache today?"

And every morning McTavish would look in the mirror and thoughtfully stroke the long silky hairs that had sprouted under his nose and along his top lip, and he would say,

"No wife, not today. Please pass me the wax." And every morning he would wax the ends of his moustache and twirl them into a neat curl on either side of his nose. The more Mrs. McTavish grumbled, the more he waxed and twirled and curled.

One morning, as he stood before the mirror, he said,

"I am going to grow the longest moustache in the world."

"It will bring you nothing but trouble," warned Mrs. McTavish.

"Nonsense!" retorted McTavish.

"Just you wait and see," said Mrs. McTavish.

The moustache grew and grew. It wasn't long before the ends could be seen from BEHIND McTavish. When the waxed curls reached down to his shoulders, his friends started making sly jokes. "How is your scarf growing?" they would ask. "Does it keep you warm?" McTavish pretended not to hear them.

Every day he washed his moustache and waxed it and curled it. The longer it grew the prouder he became, and the more often he measured it . . . the more awkward it got.

"Ouch!" said McTavish one morning.

"Something wrong?" asked Mrs. McTavish slyly.

"Of course not," said McTavish hastily. The end of his moustache had caught in his waistcoat button and pulled his head over to one side. It took him ages to untangle it. He was afraid to ask Mrs. McTavish to help, in case she snipped the end off with her scissors. He knew she would if she had the chance.

It was always catching on door handles and pulling him up with sudden jerks. Sometimes, when he was asleep, one of the tight little waxed curls would catch on the bed-post and as he tossed and turned in the night, his moustache would twist round the post like bindweed. Then he would have to spend half the night unwinding it, praying all the time that Mrs. McTavish would not wake and see him. He was quite glad when it grew long enough for him to push the ends into his pockets. The trouble was, he didn't have room for anything else in his pockets then, and his hands were always full of things that should have been in them. If he forgot to put the ends in his pockets, they caught in his bootlaces and tripped him up. One day two birds looking for something to make nests with picked up the ends and flew off in opposite directions. What a shout he gave!

Mrs. McTavish pretended not to notice. She just wondered how much longer it would be before McTavish got tired of fighting with the moustache and shaved it off.

Then one day, as McTavish was waxing and twirling in front of the mirror, there was a great commotion outside.

"A rope . . . a rope . . . someone fetch a rope . . ."

A small boy had fallen into a deep hole. There was no time to lose if he was to be saved. McTavish did not hesitate. He flung himself onto the ground and dropped both ends of his moustache into the hole. "Grab hold of that, boy!" he shouted. "Tie it round your waist." The boy's father caught hold of McTavish's ankles, McTavish held onto his moustache and together they pulled. Slowly McTavish slid backwards from the hole, slowly the boy emerged, tear stained and frightened, but safe.

Everyone said McTavish was a hero. "Hoorah for McTavish!" they cried, "Hoorah for his moustache!"

"You see wife," said McTavish as Mrs. McTavish bathed his sore face, "A moustache can be useful as well as beautiful."

"I am proud of you both," said Mrs. McTavish.

THE LITTLE CAR THAT NEVER HAD A WASH

"I wish they wouldn't park you by me," said the big blue Cadillac. "You're always so dirty." A smart brown convertible nodded. "He doesn't even smell very nice," he said.

"All that dirt must reduce your speed," said a two-seater sports-car. Ricky, the little red car, felt ashamed. It wasn't

111

his fault that none of the cars in the big garage liked him or wanted to stand near him. They were hosed down and polished regularly, but Ricky's owner, Charley Collins, was lazy and never bothered to wash the dirt from him or even clean his windows properly. The little red car had never had a wash in his life! Whenever he was put back in the garage Ricky felt unhappy, for all the other cars tried to edge away from him and made remarks about how dirty he was.

One day, Charley Collins was driving in the town when suddenly there was a loud bang. The little red car stopped. He felt all lopsided. One of his tyres had burst. "Oh, darn!" said Charley. "I expect there was a nail in the road." As there was a garage close by, Charley drove the little car, limping, into the garage and asked a mechanic to put on a new tyre. "You need four new tyres, not one," said the mechanic,

walking round Ricky. "They're all worn down to the treads."
Charley grumbled at having to buy four new tyres, but he
had to agree that they were necessary.

The mechanic set to work and put on four brand-new tyres.
Ricky could see himself in the garage mirror and he was
thrilled. "I've got FOUR new shoes!" he told himself proudly.
"You're carrying a mighty lot of dirt around with you,"
remarked the mechanic. "Why not put your car through the
car-wash?" He pointed to a sign that said CAR WASH —
ENTRY. "It'll only take you a few minutes to go through —
washed, waxed and dried."

"Okay!" said Charley. "Put a car-wash on the bill." Getting
into the little red car, he drove him into the car-wash. Then
began the most exciting experience Ricky had ever had.

Great fountains of water suddenly spouted all over him.
He puffed and blew, quite taken by surprise. The water

sluiced all over him and down his windows. Then, almost before he could draw breath, two enormous rollers came flapping out from somewhere and began to tickle him. Ricky wriggled and squirmed and laughed. He'd never enjoyed anything so much in his life.

The rollers dried him all over thoroughly from roof to

114

chassis, and then a waxy substance shot out and polished him until he felt smooth and sleek.

When at last he glided out of the car-wash he looked like new. Charley climbed out to pay his bill, then stopped and gazed in astonishment.

"I'll be darned if that isn't worth paying for!" he cried. "I didn't know I'd got such a smart car. I'm real proud of you!" Ricky laughed. He was proud too! Looking at himself in the garage mirror before he left, he hardly knew himself. "This won't be your last wash," said Charley. "I'm going to take you along to that car-wash every week."

When the other cars in the big garage saw Ricky, they could hardly believe their eyes. The big blue Cadillac blinked his headlamps in amazement. "Whatever's happened to you?" he demanded. "I thought for a minute you were a new car." "You do look smart," admitted the brown convertible. "I've been through a car-wash," explained Ricky. "You've got new tyres too," said the sports-car. "Come and stand next to me," said the Cadillac. "I'm always washed by hand and hose myself. Do tell me what happens in a car-wash. I'd love to go through. It must be quite an adventure."

Ricky sighed happily. He wasn't an outcast any more, and wouldn't be again, for from now on, Charley Collins had promised, he'd have a wash every week!

116

THE MOONLIGHT PICNIC

Wherever was Teddy? He had been lying by Miranda's side when she went to sleep. Now he was gone!

Miranda jumped out of bed. No, he hadn't fallen out! Then, through the window in the moonlight, she saw him. He was hurrying across the lawn towards the woods.

Miranda opened the window and called, "Teddy, come back!"

But Teddy took no notice. Miranda slipped on her dressing-gown and slippers and hurried downstairs and out through the front door. She was just in time to see Teddy disappear into the woods.

She broke into a run. The words of a song, 'The Teddy Bears' Picnic' to which she had listened on a record-player just before bedtime, flashed into her mind:—

If you go down to the woods today you're sure of a
big surprise;

If you go down to the woods today you'd better go
in disguise.
Dare she go into the woods — They looked gloomy, but her
Teddy had gone in, and he belonged to her.
"I'm going in," she said bravely, and ran on to the path.
Suddenly a huge Teddy Bear stepped out from the trees

with hand raised. "Stop!" he said. "Nobody is allowed in the woods on the night of the Teddy Bears' picnic."

"So that's what it is!" said Miranda. "Well, I'm going to look after my Teddy!"

The giant bear let out a loud, angry growl as Miranda darted past him and ran into the trees. "Come back!" he

119

shouted.

Miranda took no notice. She ran on until suddenly she came on the picnic site. She climbed up a tree and lay still on one of the branches. Below her Teddy Bears sat in a circle, in the middle of which was a big bear with a crown on his head.

'He must be the King of the Bears,' thought Miranda.

The King of Bears stood up, raised his hand, and said, "Welcome to Teddy Bears from everywhere! We meet only once a year. Time is short. Let us feast!"

Two Teddy Bears wearing aprons began to hand out food and drink to the other Teddy Bears. There were pots of honey, which every bear grasped at eagerly. They had no spoons; they just stuck their paws into the pots and sucked the honey from them. They ate cream cakes and all kinds of sugary titbits.

Miranda was thinking of calling out to her Teddy not to eat so many cream cakes, when there came a commotion from the woods. There was a crashing sound as a large body blundered through thick undergrowth. Then the huge bear who had stopped her burst into the circle.

"A stranger — a little girl — ran past me," he panted. "She has come to spy on us —". He broke off suddenly. Miranda was just about level with his eyes. He pointed at her. "There she is! Catch her!"

Surprised and alarmed, Miranda turned to climb down from the tree, but she missed her footing and tumbled from the branch — down . . . down . . . down.

She shut her eyes when she felt herself falling. When she opened them she found she was on the floor by her bed.

"Oh!" she cried. "I've fallen out of bed!"

She looked up. There was her Teddy Bear, lying in his usual place by her pillow.

120

"How silly!" she said "I heard that record and I must have dreamed I'd gone to the Teddy Bears' picnic."

She climbed back into bed, shaking her head. "It couldn't be," she murmured, but when she fell asleep, she was still wondering. She'd noticed that Teddy had a streak of cream over his mouth. There was a smile on his face, and — yes — there were cake crumbs on his lips!

121

A TUG-O-WAR

All was peaceful in the forest. The birds were singing, animals were grazing, butterflies were flitting. Mother Sparrow was sitting on her nest waiting for Father Sparrow to bring her a worm. Father Sparrow was at the waterhole.

"Move over Mr. Crocodile," he said, "I want to drink."

Mr. Crocodile opened one lazy eye. "If I want to lay in the waterhole, then I will," he said. "Go and find a drink somewhere else."

Father Sparrow was cross, but how can a sparrow argue with a crocodile?

He found a worm and took it to Mother Sparrow. He was

sitting in the tree beside her when there was a tremendous bump. The tree shook and trembled as though it was about to fall.

"What's happening?" chirped Mother Sparrow anxiously. If the tree fell, their nest would fall too and her eggs would break.

"It's Mr. Elephant," said Father Sparrow. "Hey there Mr. Elephant, why don't you look where you are going? You nearly shook our nest from the tree."

Mr. Elephant said nothing.

"You might say you are sorry," said Father Sparrow.

"I might, but I'm not going to," said Mr. Elephant.

Father Sparrow was very annoyed at his rudeness. "I'll tie you up if you dare to do it again," he said.

Mr. Elephant laughed. "YOU tie ME up, ha . . . ha . . ." and he plodded off into the forest rumbling and gurgling with laughter.

"Just you wait and see," said Father Sparrow. He flew down to the waterhole. Mr. Crocodile was still bathing and he still would not let anyone near enough to get a drink. "If you don't come out of there I'll tie you up," said Father Sparrow.

"You might tie me, but you'll never hold me," laughed Mr. Crocodile.

"We shall see, said Father Sparrow and went in search of an extra long, extra strong vine.

The next time Mr. Elephant passed by the tree in which the sparrows had their nest, he bumped into it deliberately.

"Oh . . . oh . . ." cheeped Mother Sparrow.

"I'm going to tie you up," said Father Sparrow sternly.

"You might tie me, but you'll never hold me," laughed Mr. Elephant. And just to show that he wasn't afraid, he stood still and let Father Sparrow fly over his back and under his tummy with the vine and tie it in a knot.

"I will prove I can hold you," said Father Sparrow. "Just give me time to pick up the other end of the vine. It's behind that tree." While Mr. Elephant was still laughing, he flew to the waterhole with the other end of the vine in his beak.

"I'm going to tie you up AND I'm going to hold you," he said to Mr. Crocodile.

Mr. Crocodile was so amused, he left the water and came out onto the bank. "Go on then," he said, and waited while

Father Sparrow tied the vine around his tail.

"Just give me time to pick up the other end of the vine," said Father Sparrow. "It's behind that tree."

Father Sparrow hid in the trees, and then called loudly, "Start pulling . . . NOW!"

Mr. Elephant began to pull. Mr. Crocodile began to pull. They both thought they were pulling Father Sparrow. Instead they were pulling each other. How they grunted and puffed!

"That sparrow is incredibly strong," grunted Mr. Elephant.

"That sparrow must be the strongest bird in the world," puffed Mr. Crocodile.

Mr. Crocodile and Mr. Elephant were very well matched. Neither one could pull the other half an inch!

At sundown, Father Sparrow called from his hiding place.

127

"Are you ready to give in?"

"Yes . . . yes . . ." puffed Mr. Elephant. He was so tired. He couldn't understand why Father Sparrow sounded so fresh.

"Are you ready to give in?" called Father Sparrow again.

"Yes . . . yes . . ." grunted Mr. Crocodile. He was as tired as Mr. Elephant. And he felt just as foolish.

"I'm letting go of the vine . . . NOW!" called Father Sparrow. And as he said "NOW" he cut it through the middle. Mr. Elephant lost his balance at one end and sat down with a bump. Mr. Crocodile lost his balance at the other end and slipped on the mud. They both disappeared into the forest with the sound of laughter ringing in their ears. It would be a long time before either of them were rude to Father Sparrow again!

BLACKBERRY JAM

Once upon a time, there was an old woman who liked blackberries. She didn't eat them. Oh no. She took them home, put them in a cooking pot, poured sugar over them, boiled them until they turned into thick delicious jam; tipped the jam into jars and put the jars in her store-cupboard. Shelf after shelf in her store-cupboard was weighed down with jars, and every jar was full. She had more jam than she could ever use herself but that didn't bother her. Oh no. The more jars she had to count the happier she was. She stored blackberry jam like bees store honey and misers store gold.

Every autumn she would go into the wood and pick every ripe berry she could find. Which was all very well for her, but it didn't leave many for anyone else.

One afternoon, when the fruit was right for picking, she came upon a tangle of brambles loaded down with berries. The woodland creatures, who liked blackberries too, had gathered there and were quietly helping themselves. They moved to one side so that she could pick her share.

"Shoo!" said the old woman rudely, "Get out of my way."

"There are enough berries for us all here," said one of the rabbits, popping a plump juicy berry into his mouth.

129

"How dare you eat the berries — I want them to make some jam," scolded the old woman. She flapped her apron and shouted, and looked so cross and bad-tempered, she frightened the timid little creatures away, And when they had gone she picked the bushes bare.

She was on her way home, feeling mightily pleased with

herself, when a bear stepped out of the wood and spoke to her.

"Good-day," said the bear. "What have you in your basket?"

"Blackberries," said the old woman pushing past. She wasn't afraid of anyone, not even a bear.

"I like blackberries myself," said the bear. "Will you let me have a few?"

"Pick your own," said the old woman.

"I would if I could find some to pick," said the bear.

"You should get up earlier," said the old woman rudely.

"YOU should leave some on the bushes," said the bear. "There are enough for us all to share if no one is greedy."

"Pickers are keepers," said the old woman. "If I want to pick ALL the berries, and I DO want to pick all the berries, then I SHALL pick all the berries." She marched right past the bear with her nose in the air.

It wasn't long before the woodland creatures, who liked blackberries just as much as she did, and who were more than willing to share, could find no berries at all. No matter how early they were up, the old woman was always up before them. She picked the lot. Even the shrivelled, half ripe ones.

The bear decided enough was enough, so he called the woodland creatures to a meeting.

"We must teach that greedy woman a lesson," he said, "or we will never taste another blackberry. We will give her one more chance, and then, this is what we will do . . ." And they all put their heads together and listened while he whispered.

The next day, the bear called at the old woman's cottage.

"If you will not let us have any berries, at least let us have a jar of your blackberry jam," he said politely.

"I will not," said the old woman. "I wouldn't GIVE you a jar . . . I wouldn't SELL you a jar. That blackberry jam is for ME and for ME ALONE . . . NOW GO AWAY!!!"

She should not have been so hasty, for that night, as she lay asleep, the woodland creatures crept into her garden

and into her store-cupboard. They carried away every scrap
of food they could find EXCEPT the blackberry jam. If she
wanted blackberry jam she could have it, but she would
have NOTHING else!

The next day the old woman stood in her garden and
shouted,

"Bring back my food you scoundrels . . . bring back my
cabbages, my carrots, my bread . . . you have taken
everything! How dare you take everything and leave nothing
for me . . . it's not fair . . ."

No one answered. The wood was exceedingly quiet.

The old woman had nothing to eat but blackberry jam
until the next market day, and that was a whole week away.
She ate jam for breakfast, for dinner, for tea. After a while,
blackberry jam, eaten by itself, gets very boring.

She ate so much blackberry jam, and got so tired of eating blackberry jam, that she vowed she would never make another pot of blackberry jam as long as she lived.

The following year, she left the blackberries where they grew and everyone had his fair share, which was as it should be.

134

JONATHAN JOHN HAS A LAZY DAY

Jonathan John had built himself a house on a hilly slope. It had a turf roof on which daisies and buttercups grew and a chimney made of stone. He built a shed for his cow and a sty for his pig. And then he asked the girl with the rosy cheeks and long yellow plaits to be his wife.

Gertrude made the little house snug inside. She cooked, she cleaned and she polished. She looked after the cow and the pig and she churned the butter. When the baby was born, she looked after him too. And every day, when the sun was overhead, she carried Jonathan's dinner to him in the field.

At the end of one summer's day, when the sun had made Jonathan feel hot and tired, and when his fingers were sore with weeding, he came home with an attack of the grumbles.

"You are very lucky wife," he said to Gertrude.

"Why is that?" asked Gertrude. She was hot and tired too.

"Because you can stay at home all day and play with the baby," said Jonathan enviously.

"But I churn the butter, and look after the cow and the pig. I cook. I clean . . ."

Jonathan interrupted her. "You don't call that work do you? Work is weeding and hoeing and raking. It seems very unfair to me that one of us should do all the work while the other does no work at all."

Jonathan grumbled and grumbled, and Gertrude decided that he would have to be taught a lesson before he turned the milk sour!

"Let's change places, just for one day," she said. "Tomorrow I will work in the field and you can stay at home."

Jonathan was quick to agree. Now Gertrude would find out for herself how hard he worked and how unfair it all was.

Next morning, Gertrude gave him a long list of instructions . . . don't wake the baby, boil the porridge, churn the butter, take the cow to pasture, don't let the pig escape from the sty, bring me my dinner . . . and then she went to the field.

"What a lazy day I am going to have," said Jonathan. As soon as Gertrude had gone, he stretched himself in a chair

and went to sleep. He woke after an hour and began to churn the butter. Churning soon made his arm ache. It made him thirsty too.

"I'll go down to the cellar and get myself a drink," he said. He was filling a jug from one of the barrels, when he heard the sound of pattering footsteps in the room above. "That sounds like the pig . . ." he said. He left the jug to finish filling from the barrel and ran upstairs.

What a sight met his eyes. The pig had escaped from the sty and had come indoors. It had knocked over the butter churn and was pattering about in a pool of half-made butter. What a mess those piggy footprints had made!

"Shoo . . . shoo . . ." shouted Jonathan, making more mess with his own feet. He picked up a stool and threw it at the pig, and the pig ran squealing through the door. By the time he had cleaned up that mess, and the mess in the cellar, because of course, the jug had overflowed while he was chasing the pig back to the sty, it was too late to take the cow to pasture.

"I'll put her on the roof," he said. "She can't come to any harm up there and she will find plenty to eat."

He led the cow up the hilly slope beside the house and pushed her onto the roof. She didn't like it very much. He tied a rope round her middle and dropped the long end down the chimney.

138

When he got back indoors, he tied the rope round his own waist. Now the cow couldn't possibly stray without him knowing.

"How much cleverer I am than Gertrude," he said. "Fancy walking the cow all the way to pasture, as she does, when there is grass growing on the roof."

He put the porridge pot on the fire, checked that the baby was still asleep, which he was, in spite of all the noise that had been going on, and sat down. He was surprised how tired he felt and it wasn't long before he was snoring. He woke very suddenly and was astonished to find himself halfway up the chimney, with no idea of how he had got there.

The answer was really simple. The cow wasn't used to grazing in such a small space, or one so high up. She had got too close to the edge of the roof and had fallen off. The rope saved her, but now she was dangling in mid-air, halfway between the roof and the ground! Because Jonathan and the cow were tied to different ends of the same rope, when the cow went DOWN, Jonathan couldn't do anything else but go UP. And that was how they stayed until Gertrude came home.

"Oh you poor cow," she cried when she saw the cow

dangling in the air. She quickly cut the rope and the cow dropped to the ground with a grateful moo. There was a cry and a splash from within the house.

"Oh you poor man," laughed Gertrude as she helped Jonathan out of the porridge pot, for of course, as soon as Gertrude cut the rope to release the cow, there was only one way Jonathan could go, and that was DOWN. He fell straight into the porridge pot! What a good thing it was that the fire had gone out and the porridge was cold.

"Tomorrow," said Jonathan, when Gertrude had washed the porridge from his face and kissed the end of his nose, "I will go to the field. You can stay at home. Too many things go wrong when I stay at home."

FIVE MERRY SAILORS

"I'm going for a row round the bay," said Sailor Ted one afternoon when he had nothing else to do.

"I will come with you," said Sailor Tom.

"So will I," said Tim and Terence and Tony. And they jumped into the boat, one after the other.

They each took an oar and with long, even strokes they
pulled out to sea singing sea-shanties as they went. The gulls
wheeled and circled round them and joined in with squawks
and squeals as the sailors sang at the top of their voices . . .
   "Life on the ocean waves . . . tra la . . . tra la . . ."

The five merry sailors were so busy singing, and rowing and being happy, all at one and the same time, that they forgot to do something rather important. They forgot to look where they were going. They had no helmsman to tell them when to pull to the left and when to pull to the right, so they pulled neither to the left OR to the right, but pulled straight on . . . and on . . . and on. Soon there was nothing around them but dipping waves.

"Not to worry, my hearties . . . I know where we are," said Ted, when at last someone noticed they were no longer in the bay. "Pull to the right . . ."

They did. But half an hour later, they still seemed to be floating around in the middle of the same dish of sea-water.

"Just a slight mistake," said Ted, who really had no idea where they were. "I meant to say . . . pull to the left."

"Wish he'd make up his mind," muttered Tim. His arms were beginning to ache and he felt like a drink of rum.

Everyone began to give his own orders. Some pulled to the right, some pulled to the left. The boat zigzagged across the sea like a boy who cannot make up his mind. Sometimes, just for a change, it went round and round in big sweeping circles.

"If we don't sight land soon, I shall become seasick," grumbled Tim.

"Land ahoy!" shouted Ted suddenly. He pointed to an island which had appeared, as though from nowhere.

"That's an island which shouldn't be there," said Terence, who knew about such things, but no one was listening.

They rowed towards the island with quick eager strokes. It didn't get any larger. It turned out to be a very small island,

as islands go, and a very bare island at that. There wasn't a single blade of grass growing on it. But it was land and they would be able to stretch their stiff and aching legs.

"All ashore for ten minutes," said Ted. Tim was the last over the side. "Hold that rope," said Ted. "The boat mustn't drift away."

"Just because I'm the smallest," grumbled Tim, but he took the rope because he didn't want the boat to drift away either and sat at the edge of the water with it.

He didn't miss anything by just sitting. His four friends would have gone exploring if there had been anything to explore. But there were no holes to look inside, no rocks to look under, no sand to dig into. Just for something to do, and to show they were not feeling downhearted, they sang another sea-shanty and began to dance a hornpipe.

Tap . . . tip . . . tip . . . tap twinkled their feet all together.

"Oh . . . oh . . . what was that?" cried Terence as the island seemed to heave under their feet.

"It's an earthquake," cried Tim, as everyone tumbled over his own feet and bumped into someone else. It was nothing of the kind.

145

The island was . . . WAKING UP! They had landed on the back of a sleeping whale. Their dancing feet were tickling him.

The whale opened one eye and took stock of the situation. Should he dive to the bottom of the sea and sweep everyone off? No, he decided. He would go for a swim.

He turned to full speed ahead and skimmed through the sea with sailors tumbling about on his back like ninepins and with a plume of white spray spreading out in a cloud behind him. Somewhere, in the middle of the wet white cloud was the rowing boat, because Tim was too frightened to let go of the rope.

The whale swam to within a hundred yards of the shore and then stopped swimming as suddenly as he had started.

"Into the boat, boys, while we've got the chance," ordered Ted. He was wasting his breath. Everyone was already tumbling into the boat in a very disorderly fashion not caring whose toes they trod on.

This time, they did look where they were going. A rowing boat has never moved so quickly, or in such a straight line. Only when they were safely on the quay did they turn and look back. The whale was blowing his spout and swimming out to sea.

"We had a lucky escape there, boys," said Ted.

"You can say that again," sighed Tim, Tom, Terence and Tony.

Which shows how little they understood whales, for the gentle whale had brought them home, hadn't he?

THE YELLOW PAINT POT

One afternoon, when Billy Green was walking along the lane, he found a pot of paint and a paint brush. The paint pot was standing on a post and the brush was lying across the top of the pot with paint dripping from its bristles. It looked as though someone had just put it down. Billy looked up the lane and down the lane. He could see no one at all.

"I know paint pots don't grow on posts," said Billy, "Someone must have put it there. Someone ought to keep an eye on it . . . just in case it falls off the post . . . or a bird knocks it over . . . or something." Any excuse was good enough to stand around and wait for the owner of the pot to come back. Whoever he was, perhaps he would let Billy paint a thing or two.

He waited two minutes. He waited five minutes. He waited ten minutes. The longer he waited the more his fingers itched to dip the brush into the paint. The paint was yellow, the colour of buttercups. It was thick, and oozy, like sticky custard.

Billy picked up the brush, not really meaning to dip it into the pot, but dip it he did. With the brush in his hand and full of yellow paint, he looked round for something to spread it on. All he could see was grass and flowers. Surely there was something he could paint. He looked down at his feet.

149

He thought how nice his shoes would look if they had yellow laces. Flick . . . swish . . . went the brush. The brush was wide and the shoe lace narrow. Instead of a yellow lace in a brown shoe, Billy had a yellow lace in a yellow shoe!"

"I'd better paint the other one to match," he gasped.

He didn't see the little man standing on the rim of the paint pot shaking his fist. He wouldn't have believed his eyes if he had. The little man was only five inches tall. He was a buttercup painter. The paint pot belonged to him, and buttercup painters don't like little boys dabbling in their paint.

"Paint . . . brush . . . paint . . ." he bellowed as loudly as a foghorn on a foggy night.

Billy jumped six inches in the air when the voice boomed in his ear. He didn't have time to look around to see who the voice belonged to, because as his feet touched down again, the brush dipped itself into the paint pot and began to paint.

"Oh . . . oh . . ." squealed Billy. He tried to drop the brush. He couldn't. It was stuck to his hand. His fingers were curled round the handle as though they had been carved from the same piece of wood. In and out of the pot the brush went. In and out. Where the brush went, Billy's hand went, and where Billy's hand went the rest of him followed. One moment he was stretched like a giraffe, painting leaves on the trees, the next moment he was on his knees painting faces on the stones.

"What are you doing with my paint?" boomed the voice again.

"Nothing . . . I'm doing nothing at all," cried Billy, dizzily twirling round and round a tree as the brush painted a spiralling yellow stripe round its trunk. "It's not me, it's the brush."

"Nonsense, the brush is in YOUR hand," boomed the voice.

"But it won't let me put it down," cried Billy. He tried to shake his hand free, whereupon the brush shook HIM until he felt as wobbly as a jelly. All the time the brush shook it sprayed the air with blips of yellow paint, everyone of which, in a most curious round-about way, landed somewhere on Billy.

"Oh . . . oh . . . " cried Billy. He was all spotty as though he had a bad dose of yellow measles!

"Shouldn't touch things that don't belong to you," boomed the voice.

"I won't . . . I won't . . . ever again," cried Billy. And he really meant what he said.

"Drop him, brush," ordered the little man as though he was talking to his pet dog.

The brush 'dropped' Billy as though he was an old slipper

and began quietly painting a patch of buttercups in the grass, with no hand holding it at all.

Billy fled down the lane as though a swarm of bees was after him. Somewhere on the way he lost his yellow spots and his yellow shoe and so no one believed him when he explained about the magic paint brush. HE knew he hadn't been dreaming and what is more, he never again touched something that did not belong to him.

154

LITTLE RED HEN

Little Red Hen lived on a farm. She spent most of the day scratching around the farmyard looking for things to eat. One day she found some grains of wheat. She was just about to gobble them up when she had an idea. She would turn the eight grains of wheat into a loaf of bread.

"Who will help me plant these grains of wheat?" asked Little Red Hen.

"Not I," said her friend the duck. "I want to swim in the pond."

"Not I," said her friend the pig. "I want to roll in the mud."

"Not I," said her friend the cat. "I want to sleep in the sun."

"Then I will do it alone," said Little Red Hen. And she did. She covered the grains with soil and waited for them to grow.

Before long, eight green shoots pushed their way through the soil. The shoots divided into leaves. Stems pushed clusters of buds higher and higher towards the sun. The thin green buds changed into plump golden grains of wheat. When that happened, the wheat was ready to harvest.

"Who will cut the wheat?" asked Little Red Hen.

"Not I," said the duck. "I want to swim in the pond."

"Not I," said the pig. "I want to roll in the mud."

"Not I," said the cat. "I want to sleep in the sun."

"Then I will do it," said Little Red Hen. And she did.

"Who will grind the wheat into flour?" asked Little Red Hen.

"Not I," said the duck. "I want to swim in the pond."

"Not I," said the pig. "I want to roll in the mud."

"Not I," said the cat. "I want to sleep in the sun."

"Then I will do it," said Little Red Hen. And she did.

"Who will make the flour into bread?" asked Little Red Hen.

"Not I," said the duck. "I want to swim in the pond."

"Not I," said the pig. "I want to roll in the mud."

"Not I," said the cat. "I want to sleep in the sun."

"Then I will do it," said Little Red Hen. And she did.

The wheat was ground into flour. The flour was made into bread.

"Who will help me eat the bread?" asked Little Red Hen.

"I will," said the duck. "I have finished swimming in the pond."

"I will," said the pig. "I have finished rolling in the mud."

"I will," said the cat. "I have finished sleeping in the sun."

"Oh no, you won't," said Little Red Hen. "I found the grains of wheat. I cut the wheat when it was ready. I ground the ripe wheat into flour. I made the flour into bread, and so I am going to eat the bread myself."

And so she did.

HOW THE KING'S TEA WAS SPOILT

Small Peter had a pet white mouse. It had a little pink nose, two pink eyes and twitching whiskers, and it lived in Small Peter's pocket. Small Peter worked as a kitchen boy in the castle on the hill. He ran errands for the cooks and filled milk jugs and cleaned spoons. His work kept him busy, but not so busy that he did not have time to play with Cuthbert now and then, and feed him little pieces of cheese.

No one knew about the mouse in Peter's pocket, so no one worried about it. You may be sure that if they had known they WOULD have worried. Cooks do not like mice. They are afraid the mice will run up their white aprons and crawl under their tall white hats and tickle their bald heads. They are also afraid they will eat all the food. The King loved to be served tea and special cakes every afternoon.

One day, when all the cooks were busy stirring and beating and chopping and mixing, Small Peter crawled under the big kitchen table and took the mouse from his pocket.

"Would you like a piece of cheese Cuthbert?" he asked. Cuthbert was NOT listening.

He had taken one look at all the legs and feet standing around the table, and panicked.

161

"Come back . . ." whispered Peter. But it was too late.

"EEEK! screeched one of the cooks. "It's a mouse!" He leapt on to the table and put his foot into a bowl of batter.

"EEEK!" screeched all the other cooks. Small Peter stared in amazement. The cooks were jumping about like jumping beans.

They all ended on the table and not one of them looked where he was putting his feet. The King's tea was spilt, trodden in and crumbled. No one except Small Peter seemed to notice.

"Don't be silly," said Small Peter. "He's only a little mouse. You'll frighten him with all this shouting."

"Are you responsible for this, boy?" demanded the Head Cook, who had one foot in a chocolate sponge and the other in a dish of cold custard.

Small Peter trembled, ever so slightly.

"Well . . . it is my mouse," he said.

"THEN REMOVE IT!" thundered the Head Cook.

"Y . . . ye . . . yes sir," said Small Peter. But finding a frightened mouse in a kitchen full of frightened cooks isn't easy. Every time one of the cooks THOUGHT he saw the mouse, he threw something at it. It positively rained custard and carrots and eggs. The mouse stayed well hidden. Not one of the cooks could throw straight, but sooner or later something was bound to hit him.

"Cuthbert, where are you?" called Small Peter as he crawled about on his knees. He found him, at last, behind a cupboard.

"GET . . . " began the Head Cook.

"Shush!" said Small Peter, quite forgetting that he was speaking to the most important cook in the kitchen. "If you want him to come out, you'll have to give him a piece of cheese." And then, because the Head Cook HAD shushed, and was shushing everyone else too, Small Peter said boldly, "I'll get him some."

There was nothing the Head Cook could do, except try not to shout, as Small Peter went to the larder and took out the very best piece of cheese.

"There . . . " said Small Peter as the mouse sat on his hand nibbling the cheese the Head Cook had been saving for the King. "Isn't he sweet? He wouldn't harm anyone."

"GET . . . " The Head Cook's shout turned to a whisper. " . . . him out of my kitchen . . . please . . . "

"Righty . . . ho . . . " said Small Peter and carried Cuthbert home.

And that is why, one Friday afternoon, the King had toast and jam for his tea instead of cakes and jellies and flans, and why, after that day, the mouse stayed at home when Small Peter went to work in the kitchen.

THE BALLOON WITH A FACE

Timothy was out shopping with his grandmother when he saw a man selling balloons. They were beautiful; one had a face! Timothy was delighted when Granny said, "Which one would you like, Tim?" It just had to be the one with a face.

"Hold tight," advised the man. "It's very frisky!" It certainly was. It jerked on Tim's hand all the way home.

Indoors, Timothy noticed something strange. The balloon's face wasn't smiling — it was sad. That night he tied his balloon to the bedpost. "Goodnight, Mr. Balloon!" he said, "Be happy!" Later, Timothy awoke. His balloon was tugging at the string. He tried to tighten it but the balloon pulled harder. Before Tim could let go, he was sailing out of the window!

167

"Wow!" yelled Tim. "Please put me down!" He looked up at the balloon. The face was smiling. "Oh, I'm glad you're happy again — but I'm not! At least, I don't think I am. Oh, please, do put me down!"

The face opened its mouth and spoke: "Can't stop, Timothy. It's just not possible. This is my chance. Thank you for undoing the string." Tim tried to explain: "I was tying it tighter!" The face laughed. "Never mind! You set me free, Timothy! Free! YOU mustn't start being unhappy. You're my friend and I'm taking you on a splendid adventure. So, hold tight . . . here we go!"

Down below, houses and trees looked like little blobs. A bird came up calling, "Whooo . . . are . . Youooo?" He tickled Tim's toes with his wing feathers. "Please don't do that to my feet, it makes me giggle," said Tim. The owl laughed, "Hooo! Hooo!" and went swooping down as they sailed up and up.

"Get ready, Tim!" said the face. "We're going to jump right over the church spire . . . One, two, three . . . Now!" The balloon swayed as Timothy pulled up his knees. "Whee!" he cried. "That was exciting! What next! Is there anything else?" The balloon was glad that Tim was enjoying himself. "You have no idea," he said, "what wonderful things we shall do!"

168

It was marvellous soaring through the dark blue sky, seeing the stars come out, more and more every minute. "We're very high, aren't we?" said Tim. "Not really," replied the face. "We're going much higher. You'll see!"

Just then, the moon came riding out from behind a cloud. "Hallo there!" shouted the face looking up. "Shan't be long now! I'm on my way at last!" Timothy was amazed; he had to think what the face meant.

"Please," he asked, "where, exactly, are you going?" The face gave a grin. "Why, to visit my friend The Man in the Moon, of course! He invited me ages ago. He'll be delighted to see you."

Timothy had another quiet think. "Does he like children, then?" he asked. The balloon was humming to himself. "Hmm, hmm, hmm! . . . Hmm, tiddly hmmm! LIKE children? He loves them! He's always shining into their bedrooms, giving them a light — been doing it for years. He needs a holiday. That's why I'm going — to stand in for him. He couldn't leave the moon without a face!" Timothy agreed that would be terrible. "How long do you think you will stay?" he wanted to know. "Oh, for always, Tim. You want me to be happy, don't you? Well, I shall be — up there!"

At that moment, a plane appeared, travelling fast. "Hold on, Tim!" warned the face. "We may get blown about!"

Suddenly, Tim was turning over and over — he'd never managed such excellent somersaults before. "Look at me!" he shouted to the balloon. One old lady in the plane saw him, but nobody believed her! Then the plane had gone and the balloon, with Tim swinging backwards and forwards, slowly righted itself.

170

They stopped to rest on a star. "Well, Tim, what will your
friends say about this? . . . Oh, I forgot, you'll be with me . . .
Unless you'd rather go home?" Tim nodded. The face smiled,
"Then you shall! No trouble at all! . . . Goodbye, Timothy!"
Without another word he slithered off the balloon and
floated away like a jelly fish.

Tim called after him, "Goodbye! You're still my friend?" An answer came back faintly, "I shall always be your friend." Then Tim shouted again, "Hi! You didn't tell me how to get down!" A small voice behind him said, "Don't worry, Timothy." It was the star. Tim gazed at her. She was shining and sparkling like a great diamond. He'd never seen anything so beautiful. "I'll help you," she said. "Put the balloon up on this sharp spike. I'll make a tiny hole: then as the balloon goes down, you will go down too." It sounded too good to be true, but it worked. "Goodbye!" he called. "Thank you!" He waved to the star and she twinkled back; then she went paler and paler until he couldn't see her at all.

The sun was rising — a new day had begun. Tim could see fields and hedges. He was so happy he gave a jump to get home quickly. Bump! . . . He was there — in his own bed! Had he been dreaming it all! No, for there on the floor lay the shrivelled balloon — with no face!

Timothy ran to the window. There sailed the moon, lower and paler as morning came, and there was his friend, the balloon-face smiling at him. Timothy waved and waved. The smile grew to a big grin as the face slowly winked back at Timothy.

THE KING OF BIRDS

Once, long ago, the King of Birds lived with his subjects in the hilly highlands of Burma. One day, one of his subjects flew down to the flat lowlands. When he returned he called the other birds together.

"Today I have seen a marvellous thing," he said. "In the lowlands there are fields full of seeds just waiting to be eaten. It is foolish to spend so much time searching for food in the hills when it is waiting to be picked up in the fields."

"Let's all fly to the lowlands," twittered the birds in great excitement.

"Stay here, in the highlands, where you are safe," said the King of Birds, who was King because he was wise. "There will be men guarding the fields. You will be captured."

But the birds were so excited they wouldn't listen to his wise counsel. "We will fly in a flock," they said. "There is always safety in numbers."

Nothing the King said would make them change their minds and off they flew. When they reached the rice fields,

173

they swooped down with a deafening chorus of chirps and
cheeps and began to eat as fast as they could. "The King was
wrong and we were right," they said, between mouthfuls.

But how wrong THEY were and how RIGHT the King was.
The men who had planted the rice needed it for their

families and they were determined the birds should not have it. They had prepared a trap. The birds had never seen a net before.
They did not know that a simple looking thing could be so dangerous.

Suddenly there was a shout. Men and boys jumped from hiding places in the field and sprang the net. The birds were captured. Every single one. They fluttered and they struggled but the net was strong and held them tightly.

"The King was right and WE were wrong," they said sadly.

Up in the highlands, the King was scanning the sky anxiously. His subjects had been gone a long time. Too long. Something must have happened. He decided to go to the lowlands himself.

"It's the King," chatted the birds when they saw him. "It's the King . . . oh please help us."

The King of Birds, who was King not only because he was wise, but because he was kind as well, said, "I can only help you if you do exactly as I tell you."

"We will . . . we will . . . " twittered the birds eagerly.

When the King of Birds was sure everyone was listening, he said, "When I give the signal you must all beat your wings at the same time and rise into the sky together."

"We are ready . . . we are ready . . . " twittered the birds.

"NOW!" commanded the King of Birds, who was King not only because he was kind and wise, but because he could command as well. Up flew the birds. UP UP UP in a great fluttering cloud. As they rose into the sky, the net that surrounded them on all sides, rose into the air with them. They were still trapped.

"Fly! Fly! Fly! Follow me home to the highlands," ordered the King of Birds as his subjects began to panic.

What a strange sight it was to see a net full of birds flying across the sky. They reached the highlands safely. But they were still not free.

"Are we to stay in this net forever?" they asked one another.

"I will get help," said the King of Birds. He called upon his friend the mouse. "Please come at once," he said.

"What can a tiny mouse do against such a big net?" asked the birds sadly when they saw the tiny scampering creature sniffing round the edge of the net. The mouse scampered away and they saw a chance of escape, even if it was small, disappear.

"Please come back . . . we didn't mean to offend you," they chirped. "The King was right before. Maybe he is right again. Maybe you CAN help us."

"They had no reason to worry. The mouse had gone to fetch his relations. What one mouse can do in an hour, a dozen mice can do in a minute. What did they do? They nibbled and gnawed at the strands of the net. One by one the strands snapped. Soon there was a hole large enough for even the largest bird to slip through without damaging his tail feathers.

One by one they soared into the sky and spread their wings.

"The King was right," they sang. "The King was right."
The net lay empty and forgotten on the ground.
How good it was to be free. How lucky the birds were to
have a King who was kind enough to forgive their foolishness
and wise enough to find an answer to a problem that seemed
to have no solution.

178

THE THREE WISHES

One cold winter evening, a woodcutter and his wife were sitting in front of the fire warming their toes. They were very poor and one of their favourite ways of passing the time on a cold night was to wish for things they did not have.

"You may wish first tonight," said the woodcutter's wife.

"I wish I had a pair of thick woollen socks to keep my toes warm," said the woodcutter, drawing even closer to the fire.

"I wish I had a fine woollen shawl to drape round my shoulders," said his wife.

"I wish I had a dappled horse to ride."

"I wish I had a dress of patterned silk."

I wish . . . I wish . . . The more the woodcutter and his wife wished, the sillier were the things they wished for.

"I wish I had a golden nail to mend the broken chair with."

"I wish I had a golden needle to darn your socks with."

"I wish I had a flying pig."

"I wish I had a singing duck."

But more than anything else they wished to be rich, to have all the things their neighbours had.

"If only our wishes would come true," sighed the woodcutter's wife. She and the woodcutter both knew that wishes do not come true, except in fairy tales.

Suddenly, a gust of wind blew the cottage door open with a bang. The door rattled and shook on its hinges. The woodcutter jumped up to close it.

"Wife . . . " he said, "We have a visitor. Fetch a chair."

"Come in . . . " he said, to the little person standing on the doorstep. "Come in and warm yourself by the fire."

"I have not come to stay . . . " said the fairy, for the stranger standing on their doorstep was indeed a fairy. "I have come to grant you and your wife three wishes."

The woodcutter gulped. His wife gasped and went pale and had to sit down quickly. They were too surprised to say anything at all, though they never doubted for a moment that what the little person said was true.

"You have three wishes only," said the fairy, "so think well before you wish." And with that she was gone, as suddenly as she had come, and the door closed after her in another gust of wind and with another bang.

"Would you believe that . . . " gasped the woodcutter's wife when she found her voice again. "Three wishes . . . I wish . . . I wish . . . " The woodcutter quickly put his hand over her mouth.

"Stop!" he said, "remember what the fairy said. We have only three wishes. We must not waste them."

"You are right, of course," said his wife. "We will both think hard and we will make our wishes tomorrow evening when we are warming our toes in front of the fire."

Neither of them slept well that night. Neither of them worked very well the next day. They were both far too busy thinking. There was so much they could have, if only they used the right words when making their wishes.

The next evening, the woodcutter's wife made up the fire, then she and her husband pulled up their chairs and got ready to make the wishes that were going to change their lives.

The woodcutter's wife leant forward and poked at the glowing logs. "The fire is burning well tonight," she added, and then without realizing what she was saying, she added, "I wish we had a nice big sausage to cook on it." You can guess what happened, can't you? Her wish was granted. She had a sausage.

The woodcutter was SO angry, "You have wasted a wish," he shouted, shaking his fist. "I wish that stupid sausage was growing on the end of your nose." And THAT was the second wish gone. If you have ever seen anyone with a sausage growing on the end of his, or her nose, you will know how silly it looks.

The woodcutter's wife sobbed and sobbed.

"What shall I do . . . what shall I do . . ."

"Hold still and I will pull it off," said the woodcutter. But it was a magic sausage and he couldn't pull it off. He couldn't cut if off either.

His poor wife buried her face and her long sausage nose in her apron and sobbed and sobbed. The woodcutter patted her shoulder.

"There . . . there . . ." he said. "Don't cry . . . we still have one wish left. We can still be rich. I will buy you a gold case to put round the sausage. That will hide it."

The woodcutter's wife wailed even louder at his words.

"I don't want a golden case round my nose. Everyone will laugh at me. Oh . . . there never was anyone more unhappy than I."

"You won't be unhappy when you are rich," said her husband.

"You can be rich if you want," sobbed the woodcutter's wife, "but I am going to run away to the end of the world and no one will ever see me, or my nose again."

"Please don't do that," cried the woodcutter. He caught hold of her arm and would not let her through the door. "We have one wish left. The wish is yours. Wish for whatever YOU want."

"I wish . . . oh how I wish . . . that the sausage would go from the end of my nose," cried his wife.

And THAT was the third, and final wish. The sausage was gone. Though no one knows where it went. There were no wishes left and so the woodcutter and his wife stayed poor. They never saw the fairy again. No one ever heard them wish for anything ever again, even in fun, and in time they learned to be content with what they had.

THE NEW COAT

One day, when the sun was shining, Mr Mole popped his head out of his hole and said, "Where's this water coming from? I'm getting flooded out of my home."

"Whoo, whoo, it's the Gentle Giant," called the Owl. "He is crying so much that he has washed me off my branch."

"I was having such a lovely sleep. Whatever can be the matter with him?"

"I'll go and find out," said the Squirrel. Away he ran, up and up from one branch to another, up the tallest tree until he reached the topmost branch. The branch swayed to and fro in the breeze, so he had to cling on very tightly with his claws. He said to his friend, the Giant, "Why are you so sad? What is making you cry like this?"

"I am so cold," said the Giant, shivering and making all the trees rustle as he did so. "I haven't got a warm coat."

The Squirrel scampered down the tree and gathered all the animals around him, to tell them how unhappy and cold the Giant had become.

"We must do something before the snow comes," said Mrs Rabbit. All was quiet as everyone tried to think of a way out of the problem.

"We could plait the long reeds that grow down by the river," suggested the Fox. "We could collect all the down from the thistles, and make it nice and warm," cried the field mice. They ran around in circles because they were so excited to be helping to make the coat.

So, using sharp thorns for needles and fine grass for the thread, they started to sew. All through the day, the animals took it in turns because it was very tiring. You see, they were so small and the coat had to be so big.

Again the Squirrel ran up the tall tree to tell his friend the Gentle Giant, all about his new coat. "It won't take us very long," said the Squirrel. "Everyone is busy and working very hard."

"Oh, thank you," cried the Giant. "You are very kind. I just don't know how I can repay you." When the coat was almost finished, the wise old Owl said, "How are you going to get the coat up to the Giant when it is ready? It looks very heavy to me. If the Giant bends down, he will break all our lovely trees."

"Oh dear, oh dear," said the animals. "Whatever shall we do?"

All of a sudden, the trees were filled with birdsong. From every tree birds swooped down – big ones, small ones, plain ones and pretty ones.

"We'll do it," they sang. "We could not help to make the coat, but we can take it to him for you."

When it was ready, the birds lifted the coat high into the air and held it up for the Giant while he wrapped himself in its warm folds.

"You look after us, so we will look after you," sang the birds. The Giant was so grateful for his present that he took extra care of the little wood where so many of his friends lived.